Book I
Rampage on the River

by
Cody C. Engdahl

This book is dedicated to Laura, who believed in me.

Contents

Preface

Thank you for reading my novel. I hope you enjoy it and come back for the next one. I plan to write many more.

This work is the first of a series that will follow some of the exploits of the 2nd Michigan Voluntary Cavalry during the American Civil War. The main characters, and their personal stories are purely fictional. However, I took great pains to be faithful to the real events of the American Civil War which I describe in this book, as well as many of the real historical people who appear in my story. You may recognize many of them. You may not. Please don't let that concern you. I wrote this book so that everyone can easily enjoy and understand it, regardless of how much you may know about the American Civil War.

The American Civil War is still a controversial topic to this day. People argue over the causes, the reasons, and the conduct of both sides during the war. It is not my intention to make arguments either way. My goal was to write an entertaining and adventurous story that is also as historically accurate as possible. I am a big fan of historical fiction. In the end, I wanted to write a book that I, myself, would want to read. I've done that. I hope you like it too.

When I decided to write a historical fiction novel, I thought it best to write about what I know and my own experiences. I also wanted to write on a topic where I would have plenty of access to factual resources for my research.

I was born in Detroit. I grew up there and in its surrounding suburbs. I eventually settled in Nashville, Tennessee, where I now make my home. Talk to me for five minutes and it'll be very obvious that I am not from around here. Yet I'm completely taken by what I call the "Southern Gentlemanly Arts." I cook traditional Southern food, I am a whiskey enthusiast and an Appalachian fiddler. In other words, I'm in love with Southern culture.

I wanted to create a character that would have a similar experience. I wanted to take someone from Detroit and have him have a grand adventure here in Tennessee. Fighting with the 2nd Michigan Voluntary Cavalry was a perfect way for him to do so. The more I read about their exploits, the more excited I am to write about them. Much of their stories can only be found in the personal memoirs of some of the men who fought in that regiment.

Most of what's covered in the American Civil War is in the Eastern Theater. Even here on the Western Front, battles like New Madrid and Island No. 10 are overshadowed by the Battle of Shiloh, which was one of the bloodiest battles in the entire war.

I hope this book will help shed light on some of the lesser known events and regiments in the war. I also hope you find it extremely entertaining. Good historical fiction is like mixing sugar with your medicine. You learn some real history and enjoy a good book while doing so. I hope I've accomplished that with this novel. Thank you for reading it. If you like it, please join the Engdahl House email list for updates on new releases, discounts, appearances, and more at https://subscribepage.io/EngdahlHouse.

Cody C. Engdahl, Nashville, 2019

Acknowledgments

There's a more comprehensive list of my sources at the back of this book, but I wanted to point out some of the big ones that were an immense help to me in writing this novel.

Larry J. Daniel and Lynn N. Bock's *Island No.10: Struggle for the Mississippi Valley* was my number one source for all the historical events that took place during the Battles of New Madrid and Island No.10. It's one of the few books written specifically on that subject. I highly recommend it if you're looking for a good nonfiction account of what happened there. It's available on amazon.com

I cannot say enough about the *Civil War Podcast*. Tracy and Rich do an enormous job of researching and presenting the history of the American Civil War in their surprisingly entertaining podcast. Much of what I wrote about the Battle at Fort Donelson I learned from them. You can find them on iTunes or at civilwarpodcast.org.

The civilwartalks.com is a great forum for American Civil War enthusiasts. It's full of very knowledgeable people who are eager to answer just about any question you may have about the war. Some are authors as well. I have had a lot of help from the good people there.

Like I've said, there are many more sources that I've listed at the back of this book, some of which are the actual accounts from people who were there. Scholars call these "primary sources." It's amazing to read the accounts from eyewitnesses. It seems even the lowest private was a poet and a far better writer than me during the Victorian Era. I am grateful to those whose words reached out to me from the past. Those people live on in the pages they left behind for us. Still, I wanted to give a shout out to some of the living who have been such a great help to me. Thank you.

Map of New Madrid and Island No. 10

Date 1895. Source: David Rumsey Historical Map Collection.
Author: United States War Department. This image is a work of
a US Military or Department of Defense employee, taken or
made as part of that person's official duties. As a work of the US
federal government, the image is in the public domain in the

United States.

"The more I learn of the cursed institution of slavery, the more I feel willing to endure, for its final destruction." Michigan soldier, Sergeant Phineas Hagar, before dying in battle,1864.

"Thank God for Michigan." President Abraham Lincoln

Prolog

April 12, 1861, 4:30 A.M.

BANG!

Confederate Brigadier General Pierre Gustave Toutant-Beauregard blinked and let out the breath he hadn't realize he'd been holding. He watched quietly with his arms crossed and his mouth slightly opened as a glowing 10-inch mortar shell arced across the calm black waters of Charleston Harbor. *Hopefully, no one gets hurt,* he thought absently. His one-time mentor and friend, Major Robert Anderson, commanded the Federal troops that were held up in the fort. Now that the last late night effort to persuade him to surrender had failed, an 88-pound shell hurled towards the fortress that the Confederacy demanded was their own.

BOOM!

The shell exploded over Fort Sumter raining pieces of hot metal onto the unmanned parapets. Beauregard sucked in another breath.

"Sir?!" a lieutenant asked, standing just slightly below Beauregard's elevated vantage point.

The general exhaled, still gazing at the fortress across the water.

"Should we keep firing?" the lieutenant asked.

Beauregard was slow to turn his eyes from the fort to Lieutenant Farley. Farley held his saber out at shoulder level. Behind his saber, a battery of men stared at the general. Their hands held lanyards, swabs, and shells as they stood along a row of siege weapons. Beauregard turned his gaze back to the stone walls and let out a breath.

"I suppose."

Farley swiftly dropped his saber. A sergeant yelled "fire!" The shoreline exploded in smoke and flames. The general watched some of the cannonballs smack against the stone walls of Fort Sumter before dropping his arms and walking off. "You just had to do this the hard way, didn't you, Bobby…" he muttered.

The war everyone was talking about, had finally begun.

Chapter One: A Heartfelt Farewell

"That'll be your last mistake, Rebel scum," Carl said, gritting through his teeth with his sword in hand, as he stared down his opponent.

"So you think, you Yankee bastard," his opponent, Kyle, replied. Carl drew his head back, furrowed his brow, and looked off as if to scrutinize what his friend had just said. Kyle threw off his fencing helmet, dropped his saber, and stepped forward with his arms out, "Good Lord, Carl, you know I didn't mean that!"

Carl pulled off his helmet and laughed. "It's okay, no offense taken."

"You know I hold your father in the highest esteem. A hero of the Mexican War for sure," Kyle said wiping blond strands of hair from his blue eyes.

"At least that's what my mother tells me, although she never seems to want to talk about him much. But, certainly, you're about to be a hero in the current war," Carl offered.

"Yeah, for the wrong side," said the dapper young black man standing next to Kyle's trunks. The three friends had found an alley for one last bout before Kyle was to leave.

"Francis, you know how much I love and respect you. You have opened my eyes to the merits of your race, but I have to defend my homeland, my family, my honor!" Kyle implored.

"I suppose you have to defend your slaves too," Francis said, folding his arms which crinkled the sleeves of his green velvet jacket.

"They're like family to me," Kyle said.

Francis cocked an eyebrow.

"Look," Carl intervened, "we're here to see our good friend off, not to make him feel bad."

"I suppose," Francis laughed, releasing the tension the way only his infectious laughter could. "Just don't get your foolish head blown off while you're trying to oppress my people."

"I mean it, Francis, I want things to change. One day I'll inherit the farm," Kyle said.

"Well, you won't have an opportunity to change anything if you miss your train," Carl said, hefting one of Kyle's trunks onto his shoulder.

The three had been friends since boarding school. Kyle Bethune's family had sent him north to study. Francis Beauchamp came from a well-to-do family that had been free, and in Detroit, since the days it was controlled by the French. Carl's mother was French too. Even though he didn't look like her, she told him his black wavy hair, green eyes, and olive complexion had come from her family's roots in the south of France. He didn't know much about his father other than his mother said his name was David Smith and that he had been lost in the Mexican War.

All three boys had just started their university studies. Carl and Francis were going to study law. Kyle was going to study commerce and international trade so he could run his family's plantation, but the war had put that on hold. Many of the Southern students were leaving for home, some to fill the ranks of the Confederate Army. Kyle, an expert horseman, swift with a sword, and an excellent shot with a pistol, was a lock for the cavalry. "I'm surprised you haven't signed up yourself, Carl?"

"Are you kidding? My mom wouldn't hear of it. She says she's already lost a husband, she's not about to lose a son to such folly. Plus, it's not my fight. I still don't understand what it's about, so I'm certainly not going to get myself killed over it," Carl said, as they came to a stop at the entrance to Kyle's passenger car on the train.

"I would sign up in a heartbeat if they allowed me," Francis declared.

"Francis, you don't even like to get your hands dirty. Imagine you, in your fancy clothes, sleeping out in the woods with all those bugs," Carl chided him playfully.

"Hey, I'm not as much of a dandy as you think!" Francis said, slapping Carl on the arm.

"I'm glad you can't," Kyle said more seriously, as he put his hand on Francis's shoulder. "I would hate to have to fight against either of you or for anything to happen to you."

"Hey, you just look out for yourself, you big dummy," Francis smiled.

WHEEEEEEEEEEEEEEET!

The train whistle blew as a bellow of steam rolled past the friends. "I guess I should be going," Kyle said dropping his bag and throwing his arms around Carl and Francis. He stepped aboard the train as it started to crawl along. He found a window to lean out from and waved once more to his friends, "I'll write!"

"Better yet, send me naked pictures of your sister!" Carl yelled out, cupping his hand around his mouth.

"What?!" Kyle called out, but then he saw Francis swat Carl's arm, and that was enough to tell him he didn't want to know. Instead, he shrugged, smiled, and waved again. Carl and Francis waved and watched the train pull away until a cloud of steam blocked their view. The steam cleared, revealing the menacing figure of Klaus Schmidt and his two stone-faced friends.

"Oh, shit…" Carl mumbled through his teeth.

"As crude as ever…" Klaus said unblinkingly.

"You misunderstood me, my Russian friend," Carl said, extending an open hand in peace.

"For the last time, I am Prussian, and I will not be mocked by a curd like you." Klaus gritted through his teeth.

Carl and Francis looked at each other in feigned confusion. "Did you mean to say, 'cur?'" Francis asked.

"Or perhaps 'turd?'" Carl offered, scrunching his brow as if he were trying to understand.

"Enough!" Klaus erupted, "You have dishonored my sister, and I demand satisfaction."

"Well, I certainly didn't get any…" Carl smirked which earned him yet another slap on the arm from Francis.

"You're not helping matters…" Francis hissed in his ear.

"You're right," Carl said, and then to Klaus, "Look, man, nothing happened. Your sister has a crush on me. I tried to let her down easily."

"By kissing her?" Klaus interrupted, "It's grass for breakfast unless you're a…'cur' *and* a coward."

Carl stepped forward with his hands down and open as he explained, "Look, I don't know how you do things in Russia, Prussia, whatever... but this is America. The Dark Ages are over. We don't go around murdering each other over silly..."

SLAP!

Carl's head snapped to the side as Klaus's open hand seemingly came out of nowhere and struck him. Carl paused for a moment, feeling the numb tingle on his cheek. A bonneted woman turned her child's head away, covering his eyes with her hand as she scurried away. Silence oozed through the noisy crowd. Carl turned back to see Klaus and his companions glare at him. Francis stood with his hand over his mouth. A moment of stillness endured.

Carl lifted his hand to his now throbbing cheek, "Well, I guess I have no choice now."

"Excellent, pistols at dawn then. We'll meet at the river," Klaus said, immediately turning his demeanor to a business like tone.

"Swords, I'm a terrible shot," Carl said, not breaking eye contact.

"I said pistols," Klaus came back coldly.

"I'm the one being challenged, the choice is mine," Carl said, not breaking his stare.

One of Klaus's friends leaned in and whispered into his ear, "*Er hat Recht...*"

"Fine. Swords it is," Klaus conceded, "I assume you know the dueling grounds across from Belle Isle?"

"Of course, Klaus," Carl said with a tinge of sadness now that the prospect of either dying or killing a man became real.

"Don't be late," Klaus said, curtly turning on his heel and marching off with his silent friends in tow.

"Are you crazy?!" Francis scolded, "Even if you win, you could go to jail for murder!"

"That's why I said swords, Francis," Carl said, still watching the Germans walk off into the crowd, "maybe I can just wound him just enough to stop him, or satisfy him with a little of my own blood."

"What did you do to his sister?" Francis demanded.

"Nothing! She's a mere child," Carl answered.

Francis cocked his incredulous smile and raised an eyebrow.

"She said she was in love with me outside at the dance last night. Then she leaned in and kissed me. I swear, I tried to stop it," Carl explained.

"Well, apparently you didn't seem to try hard enough," Francis scolded, walking off.

Carl walked home alone feeling like everyone in the street could see the mark on his face. He pulled his top hat down, bringing the brim as close to his eyes as possible. He stuffed his hands into his pockets and he shuffled his way down Jefferson Avenue, hoping not to encounter anyone who knew him.

The housekeeper had left for the day by the time Carl stepped into his family's townhouse. His mother's closed bedroom door was the closest thing he had to human companionship. He and his mother had lived there alone all his life. She told him her family owned it, and they were the ones who paid the bills, paid for the servant, and even paid for his education, but he had never met them. Why? Something told him they did not approve of his mother and had no interest in meeting their grandson. *Fewer people I have to deal with, I suppose,* he thought. They lived somewhere out in the country. Carl and his mother had never been invited to visit, nor did they ever come to call.

Carl lit a candle as the last of the evening sun seeped through the windows. He found some dry bread, cheese, and a little ham in the cupboard. Carl dipped the bread into a glass of wine and stared at the old curved sword that hung over the fireplace. *Did that belong to my dad?* No, it couldn't have. The only thing his mother would tell him about his father, other than he was just like him every time he misbehaved, was that he fell in Mexico and all his possessions were lost with him. Carl pulled the old saber from the wall. It had fallen into disuse once he outgrew playing with it as a boy. He got a cloth, some oil, and a whetstone and began working on the blade. He could hear the creak of his mom's door. The smell of incense, absinthe, as well as the glow and warmth of candles, rolled in around him. "You will have no need of that where you're going," his mother said, her accent still strong from her native French.

"Have you been praying to the devil again, Mother?" Carl turned and gave her the mischievous smile that always drove her crazy.

"I've been conversing with the dead, as you well know." Claudette was still a beautiful woman. She stood there in her long sleeping gown, her wild silver-streaked black hair was backlit from the candles in the room behind her.

"Any news from Father?" Carl said, knowing he was provoking her.

"You are not going off to fight some fool's war!" she snapped.

"Trust me, I want nothing to do with it," Carl said, looking down at the sword.

"You're in trouble…It's about a girl…you're fighting a duel!" Claudette brought her hand up to her mouth in horror.

"How do you know these things?" Carl said, truly stunned.

"*Oh mon Dieu, ce fils à moi!*" She gasped, "You are just like your father!"

"How so, Mother?" Carl stood up demanding.

"Now you will abandon me too," she sobbed and retreated into her room with a slam of the door.

"Mother, please?" Carl pleaded with his head against her door. The only response he got was soft sobbing from inside.

TAP, TAP, TAP

The tapping on the window startled Carl from his sleep. He was sitting in a chair with the saber on his lap and empty wine glass at his side. The candle had burned itself out.

TAP, TAP, TAP

A candle outside illuminated the dark face that was peering through the window. Carl let out a sigh and walked to the door. "Francis, what are you doing here?"

"You're a boorish fool for getting yourself into this mess, but you still need a second," Francis said.

"Jesus, what time is it?" Carl asked, scratching himself.

"We have an hour before sunrise. You better make yourself presentable. Duels are formal affairs," Francis replied. Francis looked more suited for a fox hunt than a duel in his riding boots, short coat, and top hat.

"Give me a minute," Carl mumbled. After a quick wash and shave, the two young men made their way to the river. Both knew the out-of-sight patch of land on the shore of the Detroit River. For generations, gentlemen visited this patch to settle matters of honor. The two friends could see the glow of lanterns in the twilight through the trees that separated the shore from the road.

Klaus and his two friends, Dieter and Hans, were speaking quietly in German with each other. As sons of German immigrants, they were inseparable and seemed to have taken on an "us versus them" attitude with all the other boys. This typically manifested itself in sneering disdain with which Klaus now regarded Carl and Francis as they approached. "Ah, on time. I see you brought your negro. Have you no friends to be your second?"

"Why you…," Francis sputtered, "My family has lived here freely before any of you swine-hearted, kraut-stinking, sausage sucking sons of…"

Carl put a hand on Francis's chest cutting him off mid-rant. Klaus raised an eyebrow in surprised amusement.

"You know very well that Francis is my friend and is probably the best man here," Carl said.

Klaus shrugged his shoulders, pushing his lower lip into his upper lip, "Perhaps…are you ready?"

Carl pulled out the saber he carried rolled in a blanket and stood in the *en garde* position. The Germans laughed. "What?" Carl asked, dropping his sword arm.

"We are gentlemen," Klaus chuckled, "we don't hack at each other like common butchers."

"What was I supposed to bring?" Carl asked.

"Certainly not that rusty old thing," Klaus laughed. The smile vanished as he turned to his second, "Dieter, *die box, bitte*." Klaus's redheaded, freckled friend came forward with a polished walnut box. Inside the box, lying on blue velvet, were two elegant swords. They had thin straight blades that came to a needle point. Small silver cups, crossbars, and knuckle guards that ran from the cup to the pommel protected the handles that were wrapped in silver wire.

"Foils?" Carl asked.

"Well, small swords we call them. They are for this very purpose," Klaus answered.

"They're beautiful," Carl stated.

"Thank you, they've been in my family for generations," Klaus said, taking a moment to gaze at them with Carl. "If you are ready, select one and prepare to defend yourself."

"I suppose it's too late to say, I'm sorry?" Carl asked picking up one of the swords.

"When it comes to the honor of a lady, yes, I must have satisfaction," Klaus replied.

"Rule 10 of the *Code Duello*," Dieter stated.

"He talks," Francis said, raising his eyebrows in surprise.

"You Germans are insufferable," Carl said, testing the weight and balance of his sword.

Klaus pulled the remaining sword from the box. Dieter snapped the box shut, turned on his heel, and retreated to the sideline where Hans and Francis stood to witness the fight. Klaus sank into his stance, his sword, which he held lightly like a long plumed pen, pointed at Carl.

"Are you ready, sir?" Klaus asked.

"I guess," Carl said, once again assuming the *en garde* position.

"*En Garde!*" Klaus exclaimed.

"He's going to alert the whole neighborhood," Francis spoke softly to Hans. Hans turned to him, regarded him blankly, and then turned back to watch the duelers. The first beam of light crept through the trees and sparkled on the blades of the swords and on the water that ran along beside them. There was a moment of stillness, and then a step forward from Klaus, a step back from Carl. The swords tapped, and then the sounds of the steel blades sliding softly along each other could be heard.

The two men moved back and forth cautiously, feeling each other out, occasionally tapping their swords against each other. Then it was a contest of tightly circling their blades under the other, trying to find an avenue for attack.

"This is going to take all morning," Francis murmured. This time Hans didn't even bother to regard him.

Klaus was the first to strike. He propelled himself forward with a thrust. Carl countered by rolling his wrist to the left and deflecting Klaus's blade. Then he thrust forward to attack the space that was now open on Klaus's chest. Klaus rolled his wrist to the right, diverting Carl's blade. Carl circled under Klaus' blade to renew his attack. Klaus rolled his blade to the right to deflect that attack as well.

Klaus took a step back. Both men took a breath and returned to advancing and retreating, tapping blades, testing distances, and measuring each other's defenses. A few more volleys of quick thrusts, parries, and counter-thrusts went by. Klaus, impatient with the stalemate of slight attacks and counters, charged holding his sword straight out like a lance hoping to overpower Carl. Instead, he lost his footing in his hurried attempt to bridge the distance between the point of his blade and Carl's chest.

Klaus desperately tried to recover his balance. Carl, realizing the opportunity, switched from a retreat to his own furious attack. Klaus frantically blocked

Carl's thrusts while trying to regain his balance as he stumbled backward.

Carl saw him lose that balance. He lunged in, fully committing his body to the attack. Klaus's blue eyes went wide in panic as he fell backward. His sword arm now extended backward in an attempt to catch his balance instead of defending himself. Instead, he brought up his empty left to try to stop Carl's blade from running him through. Carl's blade, with the full weight of his body behind it, pushed right through Klaus's open hand and punctured his chest.

"Gaaaaaaa!" Klaus let out, as he fell to the ground, arching and twisting his body in agony. His left arm was now pinned to his chest by Carl's blade. Blood trickled out from under his vest and started to stain the white sleeve of his shirt.

Francis sucked in a hissing breath with a cringe as if he felt the pain himself. The two German friends took a step forward, not knowing what to do next.

"Oh, my God! Klaus! I'm so sorry! Are you okay?" Carl ran forward to help his fallen opponent.

Klaus rolled over to look at him, tears streaming down his face. "You…" he attempted to say something in his agony. Then his eyes widened with horror as they focused on something behind Carl, "No…" he said weakly.

"Carl, watch out," Francis screamed.

WHUMP!

An explosion of pain erupted on the back of Carl's neck. His vision dimmed as he turned to see a heavily mustached man wearing a bowler and a brown pinstriped suit, holding a blackjack in his raised right hand. He brought that hand down hard and swiftly.

WHUMP! Out went the lights.

What happened next was a blur of semi-understanding. He caught glimpses in-between the darkness: Klaus's friends standing him up, Klaus reeling in agony, Francis shouting, a crowd beginning to gather. Then he was in the back of a dark carriage with just a little light spilling through the iron-barred window. The carriage rocked and shuttered as it made its way down the cobbled streets of Detroit.

It came to a stop. A key clinked, the lock released, and a chain was pulled through metal handles on the back door of the carriage. The light was blinding as rough hands reached in and pulled him out. Two men tucked their heads under his arms and walked him into a building and down a dark hall. Once again, the rattle of a brass key undid the lock to a jail cell. The men laid him down on the floor. Then there was the sound of the key setting the lock, footsteps, and then silence.

Carl looked at a beam of light casting the shape of a barred window on the floor before him. He let out a groan and closed his eyes.

It was several hours later when he opened them again. The back of his neck throbbed. He tried to lift his head but seized up in pain. The back of his neck had swollen to the point that he couldn't move his head. Instead, he had to work his way to his knees trying not to agitate the already throbbing wound. He was in jail and probably in deep trouble. *Did I kill a man today?* He wondered.

The sound of a door down the hall broke his thoughts. He tried to turn around, keeping his head in place to see what the approaching footsteps would bring. Fear seeped through him as he imagined an even worse beating. *They can do whatever they want to me…!*

To his relief, the figure that appeared once his cell door opened was not a bully with blackjack, but a rather small man with glasses and a balding head. He wore a mustache, a vest, ascot, and shirt sleeves rolled up and held to his upper arms with garters. In his hand was a brown leather bag. "I am Dr. Rosenstein. How are you feeling?" he said entering the room.

"Terrible, Doctor, I can hardly move my head." Carl got up and took a seat on the small bunk in the cell.

"Well, you're a lot better off than the other boy, I can tell you that. Let's see what we can do," Dr. Rosenstein said, sitting down next to Carl. His hands were icy cold as he rolled Carl's shirt back to examine his swollen neck.

"He lives?" Carl asked, afraid to hear the answer.

"Yes, he'll live," Dr. Rosenstein answered while probing a tender spot which elicited a hiss from Carl. "He might lose his hand, though."

"What?!" Carl blurted and then hissed in agony from trying to turn his head.

"The good news is, he seemed to have stopped the blade from piercing his heart, but it may have cost him his hand," Dr. Rosenstein answered, searching through his bag. Carl let out a groan. "You seem to have fared much better. I don't think anything is broken; there might be a hairline fracture, but there's no way of knowing. Here, take this," Dr. Rosenstein offered a tablespoon full of murky brown liquid. Carl opened his mouth and struggled to choke it down.

"Oh God, what is that?!" Carl said grasping his mouth trying not to gag.

"It's willow bark extract," Dr. Rosenstein answered. "It'll take down the swelling. Let me rub some on the back of your neck. I'm to get you ready as soon as possible for your arraignment."

"Arraignment?! Already?" Carl said, stunned.

"I'm afraid so. I think they're charging you with attempted murder," Dr. Rosenstein replied, rubbing the ointment on the back of Carl's neck.

"It was a duel…" Carl protested weakly.

"A duel that will probably cause me to have to saw off a young man's hand," Dr. Rosenstein quipped.

The first person Carl recognized in the courtroom was his mom. She was dressed in her customary black with a lace veil that didn't hide the tear that had made its way halfway down her face. Claudette had been in mourning for Carl's father his entire life. There had been plenty of suitors for the beautiful woman from the ancient French family, but Claudette never loved another. She didn't look at him. Instead, she held her chin up in stoic dignity, waiting for the proceedings to begin.

Hans and Dieter were there too. They sneered at him and then turned their heads in contempt when

Carl looked back. Plump and pretty Anna Schmidt was there too. She was Klaus's little sister and the cause of all of this, as far as Carl was concerned. Blond Curls framed her cherubic face. Her big blue eyes were swollen from hours of crying. Carl cursed himself for leering at her voluptuous curves, that even the modest grey dress her Lutheran family insisted she wear couldn't hide.

She caught him looking at her and gave a sympathetic and imploring smile. Carl's neck was too swollen to turn away so he offered a weak smile and an involuntary wink, which he immediately regretted. *I am such an idiot!*

The bailiff led Carl to a table and told him to sit down in the empty chair next to a disheveled looking little old man who slept in the other. His reading glasses were barely clinging to the tip of his nose. At the table across the aisle sat a severe-looking man in a black suit, whom Carl assumed to be a prosecutor. Next to him was a handsome man in a brown pinstriped suit and a large brown mustache. *Is that the guy who hit me?* Carl thought and then flushed when he realized that the man had noticed him looking. The man winked back with a devilish smile.

"Carl Smith, stand up, son," the judge said. "You are charged with attempted murder. How do you plea?"

Carl blurted as he got up, "Don't I get an attorney?"

"Mr. Conrad there is your court-appointed attorney," the judge replied.

Carl looked at the slumbering man with drool collecting on his vest and wondered if it were even worth waking him. "It was a duel, your Honor," Carl said, carefully moving his head back to look back at the judge.

"Right there you have already admitted to the unlawful act of dueling. If we were still allowed to flog rouges like you, I'd have you at the post right now," the judge said. "As we have it, there is a young man recovering, whose only defense to your murderous blade was his hand, that I hear he's about to lose." Carl heard a sob escape from Anna behind him. "There are plenty of witnesses ready to testify that you and your accomplice were involved in the devilish enterprise that led Mr. Schmidt to this predicament."

"My accomplice?!" Carl blurted. The judge was about to admonish him for speaking out of turn. He looked down at the slumbering attorney, shrugged, and returned his gaze to Carl.

"We will arraign Mr. Francis Beauchamp for being an accomplice to attempted murder after you." The judge focused his brow further, "I can tell you, son, it won't go well for you, and especially not well your negro friend."

Carl's shoulders slumped. Francis was only doing his duty as a friend. The judge seemed to read his thoughts.

"There is an alternative that could save you and your friend from prosecution." Carl looked back to the judge in hope. "I'm told that Mr. Klaus Schmidt had enlisted to fight in order to save our union. Your villainous acts have denied this country a hero." The judge then turned to the other table, "Deputy Newman!" The tall, handsome, mustached man stood up and buttoned his suit jacket. "You say this young man can handle a sword."

"Yes, Your Honor, and he has a hard head," Chester Newman answered with a smile, "I had to hit him twice just to knock him out." A murmur of laughter swept across the room. Newman turned to Carl and gave him another wink.

The judge turned to Carl, "How are you with a gun?"

"Terrible, sir...I mean Your Honor," Carl Stammered.

"Can you ride?" the judge asked.

"Fairly, Your Honor," Carl offered.

"Deputy Newman, I suppose you'll be changing titles soon...can you make use of this ne'er-do-well?" the judge asked.

"I think I can beat some usefulness out of him," Newman smiled.

"What's it going to be, son, a trial and certain prison for you and your friend, or a chance to do your state and country proud?" the judge asked.

Carl was filled with dread. The military seemed like just another version of prison, one in which he had a much higher chance of dying. Not only that, but he was supposed to be in school studying law. Maybe he could read law books in prison, but then he thought about Francis. Prison meant something completely different for a black man. Foppish Francis couldn't even stand getting dirt under his fingernails. He was built more for dancing than breaking rocks. Francis had put aside his own better judgment to stand beside Carl when he needed him. Now he would be ruined for it.

"I'll join," Carl said. He could hear a sob now escaping from his mother somewhere in the crowd behind him.

"Excellent!" the judge said, "Deputy Newman, I release Mr. Smith into your custody. Please conduct him to Fort Wayne. See to it that he lives up to his end of the bargain and does not abscond." Newman gave a curt nod and moved towards Carl. "Young man," the judge continued, "go with God, and make your country and the State of Michigan proud."

WHACK!

The gavel fell and the room exploded in multiple conversations. Deputy Newman led Carl down the aisle. Carl looked at his mother. She didn't look back. Instead, she looked off towards the front of the room ignoring him. Tears rolled down her cheek. Carl then looked to the three Germans: Hans, Dieter, and Anna. Anna shuddered with sobs as she sniffed and looked imploringly to Carl. Hans and Dieter just glared.

Chapter Two: In the Army Now

Carl hissed in pain as Deputy Newman put his hand on the back of his neck as they stepped out of the courthouse. "Oh, sorry, son," Newman said with humor, "I guess you're still a little tender." Newman held onto Carl's upper arm instead. Once again, Carl felt everyone was watching him as the two made their way down Jefferson Avenue towards the fort.

Fort Wayne had been built 20 years before. It was built to defend the city against another British invasion from Canada. That invasion never came. Now the star-shaped fort with its high cedar walls, and earthen ramparts, was used as a mustering point for new recruits entering into the military. Carl could hear sergeants barking orders and the clomping of boots marching in-step from behind the wall. A brass band was playing "John Brown's Body." He could also hear the distant crackling of musket fire.

"My things, what about getting my things?" Carl asked weakly.

"We'll give you new things soon enough," Newman said, returning the salute two sentries snapped at him as they approached the entry. They passed through a tall wooden gate into a dark brick tunnel. Daylight from the other end lit the way. The sounds and sights from inside the fort became clearer as they made their way through.

The tunnel opened into a large parade ground humming with activity. Hundreds of men marched in formations as sergeants shouted and used sticks to keep the rows and columns straight. Some of the men were wearing blue uniforms, others were still dressed as civilians. Only a few carried muskets on their shoulders, and even those looked like antiques. Many had wooden replicas or mere sticks. Their commanders seemed to be more concerned with their footwork than the clothes they wore or the weapons they carried.

CRACK!

The sharp crack of muskets caused Carl to turn his head a little too quickly and then cringe in pain. On the right side of the field, about 20 men drilled with muskets. They moved in unison to the commands of their sergeant who barked out each step.

"Prepare to load…! Load!"

The men placed the butts of their muskets on the ground.

"Retrieve cartridge!"

The men moved their right hands to the leather cartridge bags on their hips and pulled out little paper bags. They then put the tips of the bags into their mouths.

"Tear cartridge!"

The men bit off the ends of their bags and spit them on the ground.

"Charge cartridge!"

They then dumped the black powder from the bags into the muzzles of their guns, ending with the lead balls, that had been packaged in with the powder, sitting on top of the muzzles. They held the balls there in place with their left-hand index fingers.

"Draw rammer!"

The men pulled out long metal rods that ran underneath the barrels and placed the heads of them on the balls.

"Ram cartridge!"

The men shoved the rammers into the barrels, pushing the balls and the powder all the way down to the bottom of the barrels.

"Return rammer!"

They pulled the rods out and slid them back into the slots made for them along the barrels.

"Prime!"

The men lifted their guns and pulled the hammers back to a half-cocked position. They pulled out small brass caps that came from a second pouch attached to their belts and placed them on the nipples, just below the half-cocked hammer.

"Shoulder arms!"

Once done with all these steps, the men returned their guns to the starting position, which was resting them against their right shoulders with the butts cradled in their right hands. Some of the men still fumbled with their weapons as they had fallen behind the others.

"Every second of delay could cost you your...and your buddy's life," the sergeant reminded them, as the embarrassed recruits finished their tasks and brought their muskets to their shoulders.

"Ready!"

The men returned their muskets to both hands.

"Aim!"

They pulled the butts to their shoulders and looked down the long barrels at the targets 20 yards away.

"Fire!"

CRACK!

A rolling crackle burst amongst the men, enveloping them in smoke. Across the way, a ramrod dully whacked against one of the targets causing a peal of laughter from the men.

"Johnson!" the sergeant screamed at the poor man who forgot to take his rammer out of the barrel in his haste to catch up with the rest.

"That's an awful lot of work to get off one shot," Carl said.

"The newer ones with rifled barrels are even harder," Newman told him, "that's why we drill. You should be able to fire off three or more shots in a minute without even thinking."

"Then why use the new ones?" Carl asked.

"More accurate, more range," Newman said, "you'd be lucky to hit a man 50 yards away with an old smoothbore musket. The new rifles can make you deadly hundreds of yards away."

"Hmm…" Carl let out, as he watched the men drill.

"You should probably start calling me 'sir' at this point," Newman said.

Carl looked at the tall, handsome man with the prominent mustache with a new beginning of understanding.

"Yes, sir," Carl said, somewhat in awe.

They walked towards the large four-story barracks at the other end of the field. Tables had been set up just outside. Army clerks were taking down the names of men looking to volunteer. Carl, realizing what it was, made to get in line, but Newman put a hand on his shoulder to stop him.

"Wait a minute, son. I want to see something first," Newman said.

Newman took Carl to the back of the barracks where the stables were. Men were taking turns riding horses on a dirt track, weaving between straw dummies. They whacked each dummy as they passed with sticks they were using in place of sabers.

"You say you can ride," Newman asked.

"Fairly, sir," Carl replied, not quite sure if he could.

"We shall see," Newman smirked. Then he barked to the stable master, "Sergeant!"

"Yes, sir!" the man snapped back.

"Bring this man one of your green brokes," Newman ordered.

"Right away, sir!" The sergeant snapped his fingers to a boy who didn't quite fill out his uniform. "Go get Claire!" he shouted. The boy ran off into the stable.

"Green broke, sir?" Carl asked timidly.

"Yeah, you know, freshly trained, raw horseflesh," Newman smiled, "kind of like you."

Carl felt a panic rising from his stomach into his throat. He had *ridden* before but typically on well-trained post horses. Those creatures pretty much stuck to the road and needed little guidance from their riders to get from one station to the next. Riding a still somewhat untamed horse was something completely different.

The boy emerged with a caramel colored horse. He had to fight to control her as she reared back when sunlight hit her eyes.

"Oh, boy…" Carl muttered to himself.

"We've been working on her for about two weeks now," the sergeant smiled, smelling the fear coming off of Carl, "but she's nothing an experienced horseman like yourself can't handle."

Newman looked at Carl with a smile, "Nothing fancy, son. I just want you to ride around the track once."

It seemed to Carl that all activity had stopped so that the men could watch the spectacle about to unfold. Carl wasn't sure if it was the fear of humiliation or getting hurt that worried him the most.

"Hop to it, son," Newman said, motioning to the horse.

Claire let out a snort and stomped her foot as Carl approached. He remembered one of his riding tutors telling him that you have to be confident with horses. They could smell fear. Carl squared his shoulders and made himself tall as he reached for the reins. The boy stared at Carl, his mouth agape, as he handed him the leather straps that connected to the bit in the horse's mouth. Carl smiled at the boy.

"Thank yo……" Carl attempted to say as Claire reared back kicking up her front legs and nearly yanking the reins from his hands. He had to dig his heels into the ground to pull her back down. "Hey, hey, hey…" he said trying to calm her. A burst of laughter erupted from the men who had stopped what they were doing to enjoy the show. Carl looked at Newman, the sergeant, and the boy, "She's a spirited one, isn't she?"

The three just watched without replying. Carl turned back to the horse. The pain in the back of his neck was on fire with all the activity. With the hand still holding the reins, he grabbed the horn of the saddle and put his foot into the stirrup. Claire's reaction was to turn away causing Carl to have to hop around on one foot to keep up. This got another immediate round of laughter.

"Hey, hey, hey…" Carl said, trying to sooth the horse.

He grabbed the back of the saddle with his other hand and bounded into the seat, swinging his other leg over her back. Claire didn't give him a second to settle, or even to find the stirrup on the other side. Off she bolted. Carl pulled on the reins as hard as he could, which only caused her to come up on her hind legs and neigh. Laughter broke out all around him. Carl desperately clung to her neck to keep from being thrown. His right foot finally found the stirrup. As she brought her front legs down, Carl took his shot at gaining control. With a little kick of his heels, they sped off through the maze of straw dummies, not quite weaving around them. Carl, remembering his lessons, started pumping his hips in motion with the horse, synchronizing their movement as one. Now he was beginning to feel the exhilaration of enjoyment. Still, it was a toss-up over who was in control, but he was riding. However, he wasn't sure how to stop.

Claire did it for him. As they rounded the last curve she slowed to a trot and then stopped just before Newman, the sergeant, and the boy. Carl hopped off a little too gingerly, lost his balance, and fell on his butt. Laughter broke out again as the three regarded him on the ground. Newman extended his hand to help him up.

"I think I can work with that…" Newman said.

"Are you hurt, son?" the sergeant asked.

"Mostly just my pride," Carl said, regarding the snickering faces around them.

"Come on," Newman said, pulling Carl to his feet and pushing him towards the enlistment tables. Carl made to get in line. Newman grabbed his sleeve and redirected him to behind the table where a sergeant was sitting and filling out paperwork.

"George, put this kid down for 2nd Cavalry. Put him in my troop," Newman said to the man.

"Ah, 'H' Company, it is," George said. "Well, Chester, you've almost got your quota."

"I've got hooks into two more, George. They should be coming this evening," Newman said putting his hand on George's shoulder. "My commission is a lock after that."

"And not a moment too soon," George said, "we've got a train to catch!"

"As long as we get there by the third," Newman smiled. He turned to Carl, "I'll be back for you. George..er…Sergeant Barth here will get you squared away. Try to learn as much as possible before we leave."

"Leave?" Carl asked, still dizzy from all that had happened that day.

"We've got a war to fight, son! It ain't gonna wait for us!" Newman slapped Carl on the back, causing ripples to agitate all the places where Carl hurt. Newman adjusted his bowler, fixed his suit jacket and turned on his heel. "Gentlemen," he said as he walked off.

Carl stood there dumbfounded. *Who is that guy?* He thought.

"That will be your captain if he gets his quota of recruits in time," Sergeant Barth said as if he had read Carl's thoughts.

"Quota?" Carl asked, still watching the dapper man make his way across the field.

"Sure," Barth said, "they don't just give away captaincies in this army, you've got to earn your rank!"

Sergeant Barth took down Carl's name, age, and where he was from. He asked Carl if he had any military experience. Carl told him no, other than shooting, fencing, and horseback riding lessons during his private education.

"You sound like quite the fancy young man. Are you going to be content with being a private?" Barth asked.

"I really don't have a choice, do I," Carl shrugged.

"I suppose not," Barth chuckled, "Chester's getting them anywhere he can. Here…" Barth handed him three pieces of paper. "Go get checked out by the surgeon. Have him sign this. Then take this one to the quartermaster to get your uniform, and this is to draw your rations."

Carl realized he hadn't eaten since the night before. He was famished. Barth once again perceived his thoughts. "The chow line doesn't open for another two hours, son." Carl's face dropped. "Make sure you get this surgeon's form signed and back to me so we can swear you in."

There was a line at the surgeon's tent. Carl couldn't believe that so many would want to join on their own accord. There were men of all ages. Some looked far too young to even be out on their own, let alone fight a war. Others looked like they could be the fathers and even grandfathers of his classmates.

"Come on in and take off your clothes, son," the surgeon called to him. Carl handed his medical form and disrobed, hissing in pain from his neck. "What happened here?" the doctor asked.

"I had an accident," Carl said, not wanting to explain all that had brought him to this point.

"Well, I think it's just bruised. We'll take a look at it again in a few days. You're awfully tan for late September. Are you a creole, boy?"

"What?" Carl was caught off guard.

"Is your daddy black? You can't join the military if you're mixed, boy," the surgeon said plainly.

"No," Carl said defensively, "my father fought in the Mexican War. My mother's family originates from the south of France. They're darker there."

The surgeon regarded him for a moment as if deciding what to believe. Then with a shrug, "Open your mouth and say, 'ah.'"

Carl left the surgeon's tent trying to gauge his own level of offense over what had just happened. The quartermaster's tent had a line too. Boastful young men in the line described to each other what they were going to do to the first "Johnny Reb" they encountered. The older men waited with slight airs of annoyance at all the youthful banter. Carl felt he agreed with older guys.

"Next!" one of the quartermasters shouted. Carl handed him his paper. "Let see…Cavalry, 2nd Regiment, H Troop…okay, we'll get you measured. You'll have to come back Monday afternoon to pick your uniform." The man measured Carl's arms, shoulders, inseam, even his head; and scribbled down the results in a record book. He made some scribbles on Carl's paper and handed it back to him. "Next!"

The mess hall hadn't opened yet, so Carl brought his medical papers back to the enlistment tables. This time he waited in the line in front of Sergeant Barth's spot.

"Ah, it looks like everything's in order, and the surgeon has ordered you a day of bed rest to recover from your injuries," Barth said, looking at the paperwork. "Lift up your right arm and repeat after me…"

Supper was splendid, at least to Carl, who hadn't eaten since the night before. It was white beans, salty pork stew, and a piece of cornbread on a tin plate. The chow line worker handed him a tin cup half full of a brown liquid with a strong nutty aroma.

"What's this?" Carl asked sniffing the cup.

"It's your whiskey ration for the day," the man said.

"Can I get wine instead?" Carl asked. The man just looked at him blankly.

The whiskey and warm food did him in after all the events in what turned out to be a very long day. Carl found his assigned bunk and plopped face down in it. He was out in seconds.

It was late the next morning when he opened his eyes. Hans and Dieter were sitting on the bunk next to him. They sat there quietly, regarding him with contempt. Hans held a package on his lap.

"We don't like you," Hans said.

"Yeah, I didn't think you did," Carl said, sitting up and rubbing his eyes.

"You smell bad," Dieter added.

Carl stuck his nose into his shirt and sniffed, "I suppose you're right. What time is it?"

"It's after 10. You missed church and breakfast," Hans answered. "Your friend asked us to give you this." Hans handed him the package.

"Did you join?" Carl asked.

"*Ja*, we are in your troop," Dieter said.

"But we don't like you," Hans added.

"You've said that already," Carl said. "How is Klaus?"

"He'll live," Dieter said. The two Germans stood up and walked out without saying another word. Carl was alone in the barracks with the package.

He untied the twine and tore away the paper. Inside were two clean shirts, underwear, his razor, comb, toothbrush, a tin of baking soda and salt, some chocolates, a small bible, $50 dollars in cash, and a note that read:

Detroit, Mich., Sept. 29, 1861

My Dearest Carl,

Please forgive me for the brevity of this note as it is my intention to get it and these few things I could muster to you quickly.

I know what you've done to save me from the horrors of prison. My heart broke when I learned the price you've paid for my freedom and now what you might pay for the freedom of my brethren. I cry in rage that I cannot take your place in this noble cause that is my own. I pray both you and Kyle survive this ordeal and that I will once again hold you, my two brothers, in my arms. In the meantime, I shall do whatever I can to help. I've collected these things, as I am told you'll be leaving soon for Grand Rapids. Hans and Dieter agreed to carry them into the fort to you. They're odd fellows, but perhaps, not completely devoid of merit. Your mother declined to pen her own letter, but I can assure you of her love. She was most helpful in collecting these things you now hold in your hands. I shall watch over her in your absence and report to you on her wellbeing. Please stay safe and try not to shoot Kyle.

Your faithful friend,

Francis Beauchamp

Monday came with sergeants banging on the iron bunk frames with their sticks screaming, "First call!" That was 5:30 in the morning. Fort Wayne was a general mustering point for all men joining the military's various combat arms. Carl found himself in mixed company of men who would be engineers, artillery, infantry, and fellow cavalry troopers. These men would be sent off to various regiments to train in their specific fields, but for now, they marched shoulder to shoulder, and some, like Carl, were still in civilian clothes.

They spent the morning drilling. The men formed into companies of about 100 each. Those companies divided into first and second platoons. Sergeants then took their platoons through various drills of marching and turning. After a while, they formed back into companies and drilled more, then as a regiment of ten companies. They practiced marching in columns and then moving into battle formations.

"Form square!" the sergeant major barked. The men rushed to create a hollow box-like formation with two ranks of men facing outward on all four sides. The first rank of men got down on a knee. The second rank stood behind them. Officers stood in space made in the center with some of the men in reserve.

"The square is the best defense against a cavalry charge!" the sergeant major shouted. "No horse will run into a wall of bayonets! Nor can their riders survive the effects of sustained volley fire! You must form the square quickly or die! You must hold the square firmly or die! Many of you will panic and want to run! If you do so, you have just killed yourself, and your pals!"

The sergeant major walked along the ranks of the men, staring them into submission. "When you see hundreds of men on horses charging at you, you may wet yourself!" A ripple of giggles made its way through the men. "You may shit yourself!" That giggle turned into a chuckle. "You may vomit on the man's head in front of you!" The chuckle turned into a full laugh. "But when that man in front of you takes a bullet to the face... you will not run." The laughter died. "When a cannonball takes off a man's head next to you... you will not run. You will stand. You will fire, and if God wills it... you will live, and so will your buddies."

After lunch, the men rotated through various training posts. Men stabbed at straw dummies with bayonets. They learned to fire muskets in nine steps. They practiced combining shelter halves into tents and building camps. Carl spent as much time as he could at the stables trying to reacquaint himself with horseback riding. By mid-afternoon, the men were allowed more leisurely activities. A baseball game broke out on the parade grounds. Some men sat in the grass to read their soldier's handbooks or write letters. For Carl, it was a good time to pick up his uniform.

"Ah, Private Smith, 2nd Cavalry..." the quartermaster said, as he took Carl's paper and then went back to retrieve a bundle of items from a crate with the name "Samuel Sykes & Company," burned into its side. "Try these on," he handed Carl a pair of brogans. They were ankle-high leather shoes with square toes.

"Don't I need riding boots?" Carl asked.

"You'll have to buy those yourself or find a corpse your size," the man replied mirthlessly.

Carl wasn't sure if he were joking so he offered a nervous, half-hearted, courtesy laugh. The shoes fit. Next, he was handed a pair of dark blue wool trousers, a waist-cut jacket of the same material with yellow trim and brass buttons. He was then handed a long overcoat, two cotton shirts, socks, suspenders, underwear, and a blue fatigue or "bummer" cap that had a short brim and a top that slouched forward.

"Don't I get a gun or something?" Carl asked.

"In good time," the quartermaster replied, "but not until you get to your regiment."

Carl stepped out of the quartermaster's with his bundle of new clothes. Men all around him were chatting and examining their new uniforms. For the first time, he felt a tingle of excitement, but then chided himself. *What, am I crazy?! I want nothing to do with this!* he thought.

"Hey, you're 2nd Cav too?" Carl turned to see a freckled face with sandy blond hair and big, bulging, blue eyes staring up at him.

"How did you know?" Carl asked.

"The yellow trim," the kid replied. "I've got the same one!" The young man said, proudly thumbing the gold embroidered collar of his uniform forward. "Charles Scott's my name, but my friends call me Chucky." Chucky held out his hand after having to wiggle it free from the sleeve of his jacket that was too big for his small frame.

Carl smiled and took his hand, "I'm Carl Smi..." Carl's voice tapered off as he realized Chucky was no longer paying attention to him. Instead, Chucky stared off at something behind him. Carl turned to see a large man in a resplendent cavalry uniform make his way across the parade ground. Men stopped to look at the officer decked out in knee-high riding boots and a stunning slouch hat that had one side of its large brim pinned up and adorned with an extravagant feather that danced in the air as he walked with determined strides. The crinkle in his eyes betrayed a smile that his mustache hid.

"Captain Newman, Sir!" Chucky snapped to attention and offered a rigid salute. Carl, not sure what he was supposed to do, tried to cradle his bundle and bend his head down to his hand in an awkward attempt to follow Chucky's example.

"At ease boys," Newman smiled. "How's the battle wound, Smith?"

"B-better, sir." Carl offered.

"I see you'll no longer have to wear your sister's knickers anymore," Newman said gesturing to Carl's bundle.

"I...um...don't have a sister..." Carl said, not sure how to respond.

"It's a joke, son. Lighten up," Newman chuckled. "I'm glad you girls got to meet each other. Let our other boys in the regiment know we're heading out tomorrow morning."

"Where, sir?" Chucky could hardly contain his excitement.

"Grand Rapids to meet up with the rest of the 2nd Cavalry. We've got a war to fight, boys!" Newman said, as he smartly turned on his heel and walked off.

Chapter Three: Travels

When first call came the next morning, it didn't seem to Carl that he had slept at all. He spent most of the night with his mind racing. Just days before, he was saying goodbye to a friend and thinking about his future studying law and chasing romantic adventures. Now he was a private in the Army heading off to war, a war that many of his friends fantasized about. They boasted about the brave things they would do and how tough they'd be while putting "Johnny Rebel" in his place. Carl even had imagined himself besting some slavedriver with his sword and hoisting the American flag over a fairly won battlefield.

But then the news of the first battle came like a cold slap to the face. Hundreds were dead at Bull Run. The Union Army broke. Soldiers ran for their lives all the way back to Washington. They left a trail of dropped weapons along the way. The Rebels were completely victorious. How could that be? Would he have been one of the dead left on the field? Would he have run away? Was he as brave as he thought? Would a random bullet care how brave he was? What made some men survive and others die when the bullets started flying? What was it like to march into cannon fire? Was fighting a man with a bayonet as sporting as the fencing he had done at school? Would his skill with a practice sword count against a man who truly wanted to kill him? Was he a coward for not joining on his own? Was he coward now? Would he be a coward when it counted?

"First call!" a sergeant called out into the darkness, snapping Carl from his half-conscious pondering. *I guess I'll find out…h*e thought.

The men of the 2nd Cavalry destined for Fort Anderson in Grand Rapids were formed up and marched through town. They loaded their personal trunks onto carts which were pulled by a team of mules that followed them to the station. A light rain dampened the sounds of men marching through the streets. Carl thought he would have liked to have said goodbye to his friends, his mom, maybe even Anna, the girl who had gotten him into all this trouble.

Off in the distance he could hear a brass band playing "The Girl I Left Behind." He looked up to see if he could see the band from behind the column of men with whom he was marching. All he could see was the big domed roof of the Michigan Central Station. But then he heard the faint sound of cheering. That cheering got louder and louder as he got closer to the station. Hundreds of people had come out in the early morning rain to cheer the men loading onto train cars. Many waved flags. Young girls fixed flowers to soldiers' uniforms. Women handed out baked goods. Men passed around bottles of whiskey to the soldiers. It was overwhelming and Carl started to feel a glow of pride.

He wondered if his mom, his friends, or even Anna would be there. He looked around at the smiling faces, searching for anyone familiar.

"Carl!" a call came from behind. "Carl!" Francis called out, as he made his way through the crowd.

"Francis!" Carl called back. Francis flung his arms around Carl and hugged him tightly, causing his own top hat to fall to the wet cobblestones. "You dropped your hat," Carl said, bending over to pick it up.

"I don't care!" Francis said, "Look at you in your new uniform! I can't believe it!"

"Neither can I," Carl said, "is my mom coming?"

"I don't think so, Carl," Francis frowned, "I think she's having a tough go of it."

"I see," Carl said gloomily.

"There *is* someone here who'd like to say goodbye... please don't be mad," Francis said drawing his lips back in a slight cringe. Carl let out a sigh, but secretly, he felt a bit of excitement and relief. "Anna!" Francis motioned to a cute and portly girl with blond curls spilling out from her bonnet. Anna stopped in front of Carl. She looked up at him with her big blue eyes, bleary from tears.

"How is your brother?" Carl asked, not really knowing what to say.

"They cut off his hand," Anna answered flatly.

"Anna, I'm so sorry..." Carl started but was interrupted when she threw her arms around him and sobbed. Carl could feel her hot tears crushed between his and her cheeks. He chided himself for being awkwardly aroused. The train whistle broke the moment. "I guess I have to go," Carl said, looking back at the men loading onto the train.

"Take this," she said, pushing something into his hand. Francis grabbed him by the shoulders before he could look at it.

"Carl, you be careful out there," Francis held him in place with his hands and his eyes. "I know you're courageous, but don't spend your life needlessly."

"I don't think I am," Carl confessed, overwhelmed with everything happening around him.

"You are more than you know. If they'd let me go, I'd come with you. I still might find a way," Francis said, holding him with his eyes.

"Hey! Kiss your boyfriend goodbye and get on the train!" Captain Newman called out.

Carl rolled his eyes, "I've got to go." He hugged his friend and then after an awkward pause, he hugged Anna too.

"Come back to me," she whispered. Once again, he felt an awkward arousal.

"Smith!" Sergeant Barth bellowed. Carl fixed his hat and scurried onto the train. The train lurched forward as he found an angle to look out the window, just in time to see Francis and Anna wave one last time. Once they were out of sight he slumped down in his seat next to towheaded Chucky. Hans and Dieter were sitting across from him. They regarded him with blank faces. Carl smiled and then looked down to his hands. There was something in one of them. It was a locket. Carl, with much anticipation, opened it and found a small portrait of the chubby-cheeked beauty that he had been so dismissive of before. He closed it quickly as if worried the image would expire if he looked at it too long. He held it with a clenched fist to his heart and closed his eyes. He was grateful.

"What is that?" Hans broke the moment.

"None of your damn business," Carl responded. The two Germans looked at him blankly.

The city gave way to the Michigan countryside. A blur of colors went by the rain covered windows. The trees were dressed in red, orange, and yellow leaves that also littered the ground around them. This, the rain, and the gentle rocking of the train knocked Carl out within minutes. He woke occasionally as the train made stops. Civilians got off; more men in blue uniforms got on. Some looked too young to be in the military. Some looked like they could be their grandfathers. Carl could see that his companions in their quartet of seats were also dozing. Chucky had a string of slobber that was clinging to his lower lip and pooling onto his jacket. Carl stole another glimpse at the picture of Anna in his locket and then closed his eyes again.

"Hey…" Somebody nudged him. "Hey…" Carl looked up to see Captain Newman leering over him.

"Captain?" Carl said, straightening himself up. The other boys were stirring from their sleep as well.

Newman looked both ways and then moved his jacket to the side to reveal a Navy revolver slung on his hip, "You girls want to do some shooting?" he smiled.

"Is that allowed?" Dieter asked, straightening himself.

Newman scoffed, "'Allowed…'"

Newman led the boys through multiple cars, tipping his hat to some of the higher ranking officers who watched with a bit of confusion, as he and his small squad of soldiers went by. The small troop made their way past all the passenger cars and through some of the cargo carriers until Newman was satisfied that they were far enough away from their fellow riders. He stopped the boys on a gangway between cars, pulled out his pistol, and shot a sign as it sped past.

"Holy shit!" Chucky blurted. Newman laughed at the startled reaction from his soldiers.

"Here," he spun the pistol in his hand before handing it to Chucky, "your turn."

"What should I shoot?" Chucky said in awe of the hefty pistol in his hand.

"Anything you like, son, just none of us," Newman said. Chucky held the gun up with two hands, squinted down the sights, and pulled the trigger. Nothing happened. "You've gotta pull the hammer back first, kid," Newman told him. Chucky, slightly embarrassed, clumsily cradled the gun, and then managed to pull the heavy hammer back. Once again, he hefted the piece up with both hands, looked down the sights, and fired.

BAM!

The blast caused Chucky to jolt back with his arms flailing to regain his balance. Carl and Hans caught him just before he tumbled off the gangway. Newman laughed, taking the gun from Chucky's hand. "You'll get used to it," and then to Dieter, "here." Dieter paused for a moment and then took the gun with a shrug. He leveled it, pulled back the hammer with his thumb, and fired, striking a passing tree. "Great shot!" Newman exclaimed, slapping him on the shoulder. Dieter allowed a smile to escape him. He handed the gun to Carl before he even thought about it. Carl looked at him for a moment. Dieter paused, and then once again, shrugged.

They passed the gun around for a while taking turns shooting whatever took their fancy. Captain Newman reloaded it every six shots using the little lever under the barrel to pack the balls and powder into each cylinder. Then he placed percussion caps on each corresponding nipple. After a few rounds of firing, Newman put the pistol away. "Hey, I want to show you guys something," he told them.

They made their way back into one of the cargo cars. Newman, after searching through the boxes, pulled out a long, wooden crate with the word "Colt" burned into its side. He dropped it on the floor, looked both ways to make sure no one was coming, and then jimmied the top of the crate off with a pry bar that had been hanging on a wall.

"Ooh," Chucky let out.

"That is what you're going to be issued, boys," Newman said with pride, "the Colt revolving rifle."

In the crate were several guns resting in sawdust. To Carl they looked a lot like the pistol they'd been firing, but with a shoulder stock and a longer barrel. Still, the guns weren't nearly as long as the muskets he had seen or even the new rifles he saw some of the soldiers carry.

"Of course, this is the carbine version," Newman explained. "It's a shorter barrel so you can draw it from your saddle and fire it from horseback."

"Six cylinders?" Hans asked.

"Yup," Newman answered, "you can load them on Sunday and shoot them all week long."

"Doesn't seem very sporting," Carl murmured.

"We can get you one of those old muskets if you insist, Mr. Rulebook," Newman shot back, earning a round of chuckles at Carl's expense.

Carl was starving by the time the train pulled into Grand Rapids. The men lined up in no particular order and marched into Fort Anderson. To Carl's relief, they were fed almost immediately: stewed beef, potatoes, bread, and coffee served on tin plates and cups. Some of the men complained that the food was not very good. Carl felt like he'd eat just about anything at that point.

Even one of the officers got into the complaining game. He snatched a fork from one of the soldier's settings, "My men shall not eat with rusty forks!" he exclaimed, as he pitched it out onto the parade ground. Carl lowered his head and ate his food while other men watched the show of the irate Captain being placated by the provisions contractors who had been paid to provide the food.

"I sure hope he doesn't throw my fork, I'm hungry!" one of the men quipped, earning a round of giggles.

After dinner, men were issued blankets and hay. They were told to find a bunk anywhere they could. Captains rounded up their companies and commandeered any vacant building they could find on or near the fort for their new home. Captain Newman scored a small warehouse right across the river, next to the Pearl Street Bridge. The men grumbled about not having beds as they found spots on the floor by the dim lantern light to lay their blankets and hay. Chucky stuck by Carl's side and made sure their beds were next to each other. Surprisingly, so did Hans and Dieter. They didn't seem any friendlier; Carl just assumed that in this new reality, the four boys from Detroit were the only thing familiar to any of them.

Bugles called out the reveille as early as ever. Sergeants shouted, "First call!" Men grumbled, as they lifted their stiff bodies from the floor and dusted off the hay that clung to their shirts and hair. Much to Carl's horror, wash troughs were set up outside in the cold air for men to bathe. He shuddered as he ran a wet washcloth over his naked body.

"At least it'll be nice and warm when we get down south!" one of the soldiers chimed. Carl hoped that was true. Breakfast was stewed beef, potatoes, bread, and coffee. Carl was beginning to detect a pattern: the same menu for every meal. After breakfast, the regiment was organized on the parade ground by company or "troop," as they were called in the cavalry. Captain Newman stood at the head of Carl's troop, flanked by two new lieutenants they had picked up from Utica along the way.

The regimental band stopped as an officer mounted a dais set before the men. Carl recognized him from the train. He was one of the officers they had passed on their way to their little shooting excursion. He was a short, thick man with a prominent black mustache. He wore a dashing uniform with medals pinned to his chest that made him look more like a French officer than an American. His boots and spurs clanked and his saber rattled as he stepped forward to speak to the men.

"Men, I am Lieutenant Colonel William Davies…" the accent sounded immediately British to Carl's ears. "It is my duty to whip you boys into a formidable and ferocious fighting force! I can tell you, I earned these medals you see here fighting for Her Majesty against the Russians in Crimea. I can tell you that it was a bloody affair. I saw many a good man cut down needlessly. Why? Because we were unprepared and undisciplined! Gentleman, I will not allow that same mistake to be made here! That war was fought for a foreign people in a foreign land. *This* war is far too important for incompetence! *This* war is for *we*, the people, and by God, we shall see our Union stand!"

Drilling filled the next several weeks. The book every man had to study was Hardee's *Rifle and Light Infantry Tactics.*

"Ain't Hardee a Rebel?" a soldier in Carl's troop mumbled to those around him. He was startled when he realized Captain Newman had heard him.

"That's right, Bates!" Newman immediately shot back, "And what better way to learn how to kill him than learning his tactics?" Some of the men mumbled and nodded in agreement. "Plus, the Army paid that bastard to write it before he turned coat. We might as well get our money's worth!" That got a chuckle from the men. "Keep the book on you at all times, gentlemen. You may get your chance to shove it up his treacherous ass!" The men broke out into a full laugh.

"Alright, take it easy, boys." Chucky raised his hand. "Private Scott…"

"Um, Captain, sir…this says infantry…ain't we cavalry?" Chucky asked.

"Yup, but before you can ride, you've gotta learn to march," Newman replied and then turned to the man standing alongside the rows of men that made up Company H, "Sergeant!"

Sergeant Barth snapped to a crisp attention, "Sir, yes sir!" the older man bellowed.

"Put them through the drills again," Newman said, and then to his Lieutenants, "let's go pet the pretty horses, boys."

"Company, attention!" Barth barked loudly. Carl and his fellow trooper snapped their heels together and straightened their bodies like planks. "Right face! March!"

Carl sneaked a peek at his company's officers walking towards the stable as he marched by. Newman was shoving the younger lieutenant playfully. It was frustrating that they had been drilling and marching for weeks but still no horses and no guns. Rumor had it that the horses were there, but the saddles hadn't arrived. *What about the guns? The sabers?*

As the weeks of drilling churned by, the men were bumping into each other less and less. The bruises from kicked heels and stepped-on toes began to heal. The blisters on their feet started to turn into callouses. The movements became mindless. The men who once moved like a mob began to move as a single-minded entity. Carl found there was a strange comfort and serenity to this like he had become something larger than himself.

The news trickled in first as a rumor and then as an announcement. They were heading south. Carl had assumed they'd be heading east as well to fight in Virginia, but they'd be going west instead. The regiment had been ordered to St. Louis to finish their training. *Good,* Carl thought, *the further from the war, the better.* Some of his fellow soldiers were more disappointed than relieved.

"I didn't join the army to guard no river," some of the men would say. Chester told them that controlling the Mississippi all the way to New Orleans was important to the Union in the overall war effort. They could cut off the Confederate States west of the river from the fight. Taking control of the river would also allow the Union to easily ship men and supplies through the waterways west of the Appalachian Mountains and deny that shipping lane to the Confederates.

"Are we supposed to ride our horses around on a boat or do they swim?" one soldier asked.

"Quit being an idiot," was the answer he earned.

The men, gear, and horses loaded onto three trains. Much to Carl's surprise, they had to go all the way back to Detroit before heading to St. Louis. He hoped he'd see his friends, mother, and even Anna. He didn't. Instead, the Detroit Women's City Club put on a feast for the men in the freight depot. After weeks of less than pleasant food at Fort Anderson, the men were overjoyed at the home-cooked meal, complete with coffee and cakes for dessert. The effect it had was most of them were passed out with their bellies full by the time the train pulled out again at midnight.

It took three days to get to St. Louis. Cheering crowds greeted them at every stop. Large meals were waiting for them too. The women of Niles, Michigan, had a large breakfast spread waiting for them when they pulled in.

"I could get used to this!" Chucky exclaimed with his mouth full of scrambled eggs. The short jaunts ended after Joliet, Indiana. From there it would be a straight shot to Alton, Illinois, where they would have to load onto steamboats that would carry them to St. Louis.

Once a day, the horses had to be taken off the train to be fed and watered. It was an opportunity for the men to get off as well and stretch their legs. They stopped on the third day on the open prairie. Carl watched men pull the body of a horse from one of the cars. "That must be your horse," Private Bates snickered.

Carl ignored him. He'd seen horses alive, but he had never seen a one dead. The creature was so big it took six men to drag it out, and still, they struggled. They dragged the body about 15 feet from the tracks and gave up. The joshing and giggling eventually died down. Only the sound of the engine could be heard as hundreds of men stood silently looking at the fallen animal.

The train whistle broke the trance. Sergeants ushered the men back aboard. "Come on, boys," Sergeant Barth said, putting his hands on Carl and

Chucky's shoulders, "ain't nothing we can do for her now."

Carl stared at the dead horse through the window until the train passed. Then he scoffed at his own naivety, "I guess I never thought they could die…" he said to no one in particular.

The rest of the journey went without incident. The men and horses loaded on to big steamboats, or "steamers," in Alton and had a pleasant ride to St. Louis. It was a four-mile march from the docks to the barracks. Many of the soldiers grumbled that they could have ridden their horses into camp if they "had their damned saddles!" For Carl, it was nice to walk that last bit after being held up on boats and trains for the last three days.

The Benton Barracks was a training camp for most of the Federal troops in the Western Theater. It was spread out on a flat field that was a mile long and a quarter mile wide. It could accommodate several regiments at any given time. Wooden barracks, stables, cooking sheds, and mess halls outlined the perimeter of the camp leaving the field wide open for cavalry drills. Centered at one end was the two-story building used as the camp's headquarters.

"You wanna stay clear of there," a trooper from Iowa warned, "General Sherman is stark raving mad!"

Carl made sure to follow that advice, only catching a few glimpses of the redheaded general as he'd storm past with his aides. To Carl, it seemed the general always wore a furious scowl that made him look like he was about to rip somebody's head off. Only once did the general catch his gaze. It was during a review of the troops. Sherman strode along the ranks with his aides in tow. Carl could feel the blood flee from his face when those hard, dark eyes looked into his. He wanted to look away, but those eyes were like black pits drawing him in, and in those pits, he felt like he could see the fires and horrors of war. Much to his surprise, Sherman's scowl broke into a smile. He gave Carl a wink before moving on down the line. Carl could feel his tension release as he let out his breath.

What the boys of Company H considered to be proper training got underway once they settled into camp. Each man was issued a horse, saber, pistol, and a Colt revolving rifle. Carl marveled at the weight of his new M1860 saber. "Be glad you didn't get one of those old 'wrist-breakers,'" the quartermaster told him, "these new ones are like feathers compared to them."

They got a new commander too. Colonel Gordon Granger had been a captain in the regular army but was promoted to full colonel when he took over the 2nd Michigan Voluntary Cavalry. He was a much more gruff and severe looking man than Lieutenant Colonel Davies, whom some had called a "peacock" for his foreign medals and "Frenchy" looking uniform.

Granger took charge of training the officers himself. He drilled them just as hard as any of the enlisted men had to endure. His ferocious glare silenced a few of those enlisted men who dared to laugh when an officer was thrown from his horse and dragged by his stirrup. Carl was one of them. Granger's glare scanned the men before resting on Carl. Carl froze in terror. Granger's expression suddenly changed from fury to surprise. Carl looked back blankly, uncomfortable with the new scrutiny from his regimental commander. Granger appeared to be pondering something. Then with a shrug, he rode off to check on, and then chide, the thrown officer.

Carl soon thought himself foolish for being impatient to get on horseback. After one day of training, he could barely walk. He had been issued a brown Morgan horse like the rest of his company. The regiment decided to issue each company a certain color horse so they could be easily identified in the field. Carl's horse was named Bess, and he was particularly grateful for her. She was calm and serene. She may have needed a bit more prodding than some of the other horses, but she didn't buck or try to throw him, and that was a fair enough trade for Carl.

As weeks went by, the regiment evolved under Granger's strict attention to detail from a clumsy mass of men on poorly trained horses to an efficient fighting force. The men and horses practiced deploying into battle lines, charging straw dummies, wheeling left and right, flanking, and rallying after a charge. They played out pretend battles and skirmishes. They practiced firing and reloading from the saddle. Carl's saber became more and more nimble as he practiced hacking at straw dummies as he galloped past.

Colonel Granger was immensely proud of the work he and his troops had done in that relatively short time. He was eager to show it off to his superior, and old friend from the Mexican War, Major General

John Pope. The two stood on a dais and watched as the regiment rode in review.

"Pope, look here!" Granger blurted to his commander, gesturing to troops demonstrating below.

General Pope was already tiring of his friend's bravado, "What of it?"

"What of it? You damned fool!" Granger admonished his commander, "You never saw a better-looking regiment, nor a better-drilled regiment in your life!"

Pope looked around the dais at the other officers, not quite sure how to react to his subordinate's outburst, friend or not. He then turned to him and said, "They damn well better be, Gordon, for I'll be putting them to the test soon…"

Chapter Four: The Runaway

Elijah made his way along the row of stalls in the stable at the Bethune Plantation. It was Christmas Eve and many of the slaves were enjoying some much needed time off to rest, cook, celebrate, and to worship the Savior they believed loved them just as much as He did their white masters. Elijah could hear the banjo, the singing, and the dancing. He could smell the hoecakes and stewed pork that made his tummy rumble.

He never understood why they didn't talk more about that fellow Moses. Didn't he free the slaves of his time? All that Jesus fellow did was get caught and whipped like a slave, and then instead of hanging him, they nailed him to some planks and left him to die. Old Man Enon said it was for his sins, *but what did I do that deserved that? What did I do to deserve this? To be a slave, something less than these horses?*

But he couldn't resent the horses. They were without sin, and to Elijah, it was just as important that they should be as happy on Christmas Eve as anyone else. So he went to each stall, spoke kindly, and stroked each long face so that no horse felt left out. He made sure that each horse had a little extra to eat, fresh water, and a clean stall.

"There you are, you damn fool!" a woman's voice broke his reverie. Elijah turned from the horse he was stroking and smiled at his sister.

"Merry Christmas, Liza," he said. She looked like no other. She wore her hair tied up in lace, a silk purple dress, and she smelled of rosewater. She was beautiful, and everyone on the plantation knew it. "Did you get a new dress for Christmas?" he asked.

Liza broke her feigned stern look and smiled as she spun to show off her dress. "Do you like it? Ms. Kathryn gave it to me." Liza was the handmaid to Ms. Kathryn, the beautiful, redheaded, freckled daughter of Mr. and Mrs. Bethune. Liza had been with Ms. Kathryn since they could remember. Both girls were strong-willed, but Liza had a mothering instinct that made her protective of the princess-like Ms. Kathryn, and Ms. Kathryn needed a confidante and ally for all her intrigues. The result was that the two girls grew up almost like sisters since Kathryn's only other sibling was Master Kyle, and he was more interested in riding horses and playing swords than entertaining his little sister.

That relationship had made for an easier life for Elijah too. Instead of working the field, he was made a stable boy, and as he grew into a very large man, he became an asset to the Bethune Plantation. The horses seemed to trust the stroke of his large hands, the soothing of his deep voice, and the softness in his large, brown eyes. They were drawn to his innate kindness.

"I brought you some real food from the house," Liza said, picking up the basket at her feet. Elijah's mouth watered at the thought of the fancy Christmas food the white folks ate. Mr. and Mrs. Bethune were back home for the holiday. The had brought guests with them to enjoy the Christmas celebration on the plantation. It was a good time for everyone. With little to do in the winter, the slaves' duties were light. The family and their overseers were too distracted by the festivities to bother the field workers.

"Why are you spending your time in here with these dumb horses?" she asked.

"I just wanted to see them one last…" Elijah dropped his eyes to the floor before he finished the sentence.

Liza put her hands on her hips and cocked her head. This time, a sincere stern look ate away her smile, "Elijah, don't you even think it!"

"It ain't supposed to be like this, Liza. We supposed to be free," he said to his sister.

"You a damned fool, Elijah!" she hissed. "Look at you! All big and fat on good food, petting your dumb horses. They got more sense than you!" She glared at him. Elijah could barely look at her. "I worked hard to get us where we are! You wanna go work out in the field like some dog!" She moved forward and grabbed her brother's arm, "Listen to me! You big, slow, and dumb! They will catch you without hardly trying. They will put those dogs on you." Elijah looked up at his sister and broke the storm inside her with softness in his eyes. Liza's eyes glistened over in tears, "They will hurt you, you…big…dummy…" She buried her head in his chest and sobbed.

Elijah didn't know what to do but hold her as she shuddered with tears. His big sister was always so tough, even the white folks were scared of her, but he had made her cry on Christmas Eve, and he felt terrible.

"Liza, Liza…they fighting right now, the white folks, they fighting right now so we can be free. I can't sit around and wait for them to decide for me, for us. Men are dying, I have to do something. Mr. Moses was a slave too. Look what he did," Elijah said.

Liza pushed herself away, "You a damn fool," she sniffed.

"When the time comes, I'll come back for you," Elijah offered.

"I'm not going anywhere! This is my home! This is our family!" Liza said.

"We slaves, Liza. We ain't family and we never will be…no matter how sweet he is to you," Elijah said.

Liza looked at him with her eyes blazing with tears. She choked back a sob and ran back to the house, leaving Elijah with his basket.

Liza wiped up her tears and freshened herself up the best she could before entering her mistress's chamber. Kathryn sat at her vanity brushing her long, red hair, "What's wrong?" she asked flatly.

Liza took over the brushing duties, "Nothing, I just get sentimental at Christmas."

Kathryn turned and regarded Liza's swollen eyes with a smirk, "You can lie to those idiot men all you want, but you can't lie to me." She examined Liza's eyes and then turned back to the mirror. "Well, if he does, this would be the best time. Nobody will notice he's gone until probably Monday. Except maybe the horses." Liza sniffed in a sob. Kathryn turned to her and pursed her lips to one side.

"Let's go riding tomorrow. We'll check on the horses and buy him some time," Kathryn said. Liza smiled and then looked down at the floor trying her best to hold back the tears. "Oh, dear," Kathryn said, standing up wrapping her arms around her friend. "Men are such fools. What would they do without us to look after them?"

It was quite apparent Elijah was gone to most of the slaves by Christmas afternoon. Old Man Enon took along some of the other slaves to search the plantation for him before the white folks found out. By Thursday, it was time to say something, or otherwise, be held complicit.

"Damn it!" Mr. Bethune ejected.

"Roger! Your language!" Mrs. Bethune chided.

"I'm sorry, Martha," Mr. Bethune said to his wife, "I just don't have time for this. We've got to head back to New Orleans Monday. There's a war on, and I have to get our cotton past the blockade before the Federals close down the whole river." Then to his overseer, "How soon can we get a tracker?"

"Papa!" Kathryn blurted.

"We need to bring him home, darling. He's got far more chances of getting hurt out there than any perceived outrage he felt here."

"I'll ride into Tiptonville, sir," overseer Johnson calmly answered, "but it's a holiday. We might not get anyone for a few days."

"And how was your holiday, Matt? Apparently, you got plenty of rest!" Mr. Bethune shot at his overseer.

"Sir, the boy gave no indication that…" Johnson started.

"It's okay, it's okay, Matt," Mr. Bethune consoled and then let out a sigh, "if that big, dumb kid wasn't so good with the horses, I'd leave him to the mercy of the Provost Guard!" Kathryn let out a gasp. Mr. Bethune looked at her and then back to his overseer, "Tell the trackers not to hurt him too much, but give him a good licking when he's back."

"Daddy!" Kathryn let out

"Just don't mark him up or injure him," Mr. Bethune finished.

Elijah thought he could hear hounds on his trail every step of the way. There was an exhilaration the moment he crossed the well-known boundary of the Bethune Plantation. He had never been off the plantation alone. The exhilaration quickly turned to fear and doubt. Several times that night, as he bumbled through the woods and overgrowth, he thought it might not be too late to turn around, to go home to the life he knew was relatively secure, even if he was a slave. Out here, anything could happen, and if they caught him…Elijah shuddered to think: a whipping? A hobbling? A hanging? He kept on.

At dawn, he knew it was far too late to turn back. He pulled out one of the dinner rolls that his sister gave him as he looked at the sun rising across the water. It was Christmas and he had made it to the Mississippi. If he followed it north he figured he'd eventually get to St. Louis. People said the Northern Army was in charge there, and a man could be free. Maybe he could help with the horses. Maybe he could be of some use to Mr. Lincoln somehow. Mr. Lincoln, the man who might be Moses come back to free him.

He knew first he'd have to get across the river to the Missouri side. All he could do now was follow the river north, and hope he found a way before the slave catchers found him.

By noon, he could go no farther. He hadn't slept since the night before. He was exhausted, cold, and hungry. Elijah gathered up some sticks and leaves and made himself a hideaway between the roots of a tree. He crawled into his flimsy shelter and helped himself to the last bit of food in his pouch before falling asleep.

It was dark when Elijah opened his eyes again. *Dang it!* he thought. *I slept too long!* It was the sounds of footsteps, breaking twigs, and soft murmuring voices that roused him from his sleep. *I am found. It's all over.*

Without moving any part of his body, Elijah tried to peer into the moon-lit night. The voices got closer, "Let's stop here for a moment," one of them said.

That's a black man speaking! he thought. Then unceremoniously, someone plopped down on top of him.

"Umph!" he let out. A woman let out a scream that was followed by an immediate round of hissing shushes. Elijah scrambled to his feet. He was quickly surrounded by men holding sticks at the ready. The moonlight only revealed their eyes and reflected dully off of their dark skin.

"Whoa, whoa, whoa, hold up!" a man hissed as he made way through the tense, stick-wielding men, "you either one ugly bear or a runaway like us."

Elijah felt some of the fear and tension ease off him, "Do you have anything to eat?"

"Man, this fool with us for a minute and we already gotta feed him," the man said to his group and got a hushed round of snickers in return. "Michael, hand me up one them hoecakes." A flat piece of cornbread passed up through the group to the man's open hand as he never took his eyes off of Elijah. "Here you go, big fella, eat it nice and slow. We gotta make do with what we got. There's not a whole lotta livin' off the land in December. Where ya' headin'?"

"St. Louis," Elijah said, not sure how much he should tell these strangers.

"Well, ain't that something! So are we, friend! It looks like Christmas is a popular time to take to runnin'. White folk are too busy opening they gifts and sleeping off they full bellies to pay any attention to any of us colored folk. I'm Jerry," the man held out his hand, "and this is John, Mike, Loretta… ah heck, you'll start learning their names as we go."

Elijah shook hands and took in the names that were offered, more names than he'd be able to remember. He was worried. He had planned on going it alone. A big group like this would be easier to track, easier to see, but then again, they had food, and there was safety in numbers. Jerry seemed to be smart and confident too.

"Let's bed down here till sun up," Jerry told his group. "Boys, pair up and spread out in a circle. Take turns sleeping. We want no more surprises tonight."

Elijah was too cold to sleep much more, only dozing off and on until the gray light started creeping through the woods. As people started rousing, Elijah could see there were about 20 of them: men, women, and a few children. "Did you all come from the same place?" he asked as they passed around what was left of the cornbread.

"Some of us," one of the men answered, "we found others along the way."

"Come on," Jerry said, kicking a few of their bare feet, "by now, some of our masters might start missing us. We better find a way across that river."

The group made their way along the river. Everywhere seemed too wide and too exposed to try to cross. Plus the water was far too cold, even if any of them felt confident enough to try to swim. From time to time, they had to scramble back into the wood line or duck in the high grass as steamboats went by. Elijah marveled at the size of them. Some of them looked like big plantation houses but with huge chimneys that poured black smoke into the air. Some of the ones headed downriver were laden with bales of cotton. Some of them that chugged their way upstream were loaded with timber and men dressed in gray uniforms.

"They fixin' to do some fightin' up there," whispered Jerry, as they watched a ship pass by full of what looked like a lot of bored men in gray. Elijah wondered if they were walking right into that fight.

The next day, the group moved through a large open field. Elijah thought it would be safer to stay in the thick tree line that ran along the river, but the majority felt they could cover a lot more ground quicker if they walked unencumbered by the briar and bramble that clogged the woods. He was hungry. Elijah stared at the ground thinking about food as they trudged on. He wondered what kind of food the liberating army from the North would have. He wondered if they would feed him right away if he volunteered to work. Then he felt it. The ground seemed to vibrate under his step. Then he heard it.

Elijah snapped out of his reverie and looked behind him. Horsemen dressed in gray uniforms came bursting out of the trees. "Run!" somebody shouted. A woman screamed. Elijah started running toward the river. He could hear screams and the pounding of hooves behind him. Loretta was running alongside him carrying a toddler. She let out a scream as she stumbled to the ground. The child wailed in pain and fear as he tumbled alongside her.

Elijah looked forward, he was fifty yards from the trees that hid the river. Behind him, the men in gray were bearing down on them. Some had already dismounted to tackle some of the runners that they overtook. Elijah turned back and bounded over to Loretta. He helped her to her feet. He picked up the screaming child and handed him to her. Her tear filled eyes seemed to say thank you and then widened in horror. "Elijah, look out!" she screamed.

A rider looped a catch pole around Elijah's neck. Elijah immediately grabbed at the rope and fought for air. The rider reared back on his horse yanking Elijah backward. Elijah grabbed the pole and with a powerful yank, threw the man to the ground. Then, arms were all over him. He punched wildly at the men. Someone hit him over the head with a club. A man shouted, "Damn it, don't kill him! We need them alive!"

Elijah lay pinned to the ground. Five men held him there. He looked up to see the man who had spoken. He was a thin, lanky man who seemed to tower over him from his horse. The man's green eyes beamed with cruelty from his clean-shaven face. He spat on the ground and said, "String 'em up and prepare to move out! We'll bring these ones back before heading out again."

They bound Elijah's hands behind his back, then put a rope around his neck that led to the man's neck in front of him and the woman's neck behind. The result was when one stumbled as they walked, they all went down. With their hands bound behind them, they could hardly break their falls. The gray-suited men snickered every time one of the lines of captured slaves tumbled down together.

"Come on, we don't have time for clowning around," their green-eyed leader said, "help them up."

One of the soldiers who dismounted to help the slaves to their feet said, "I hope you all remember this next time you get the itch to run."

"Are you taking us back to our plantations?" Elijah asked.

"You should be so lucky, boy!" the soldier responded, "we've got real work for you!"

Elijah wondered what that meant. They were still heading north. *Are we heading into a battle?* He wondered. *Will they feed us?*

Eventually, the group made their way to a clearing near the river where a dock had been built. Across the river, Elijah could see a town that bristled with activity.

Boats came and went. A line of black men was constantly unloading them. Elijah wondered if this was where he saw all those boats filled with gray-suited soldiers and timber going.

"Alright," the green-eyed leader called to his men, "this is far enough." He picked several from his squadron to load onto the rowboats with the captured slaves. The rest he left with the horses. They were greeted at the docks on the other side by more gray-suited men. Their green-eyed leader saluted one of them, "General Thompson, sir!"

"Good work, Lieutenant Woods," Thompson told him, "take them to the fort on the west side of town and have them put to work. You're free to continue your patrol after that."

"Thank you, sir!" Lieutenant Lathan Woods snapped with a salute. He turned to his men guarding the slaves, gave a whistle, and then motioned with his head to start moving.

Elijah looked in wonderment as they walked through town. Everywhere seemed busy with preparations. "They plan on havin' a fight," he heard Jerry's voice behind him. Elijah stole a look back. Jerry smiled at him. He had a black eye and bloody teeth.

"Where are we?" Elijah asked.

"I think it's New Madrid. I think they worried about them Northerners comin' and snatchin' up they city."

"Shut up!" Elijah heard one of the soldiers shout and then a thump from a club. Jerry let out a grunt from the blow. "No talking!" the soldier barked.

The street gave way to an immense work site. Hundreds of black men were building walls by taking sacks of shelled corn and packing them together with dirt. Then gray-clad horsemen rode along the tops of the walls to pack the dirt down. Elijah's group was untied and set to work immediately. As Elijah hefted a sack of corn on his back and walked to the wall, he realized that he had accomplished just the opposite of his goal. Instead of helping Mr. Moses, he was now helping the Pharaoh.

Chapter Five: The Courier

It was Valentine's Day. Kyle read the letter again. It was the only thing keeping him warm while he stood on the parapets that overlooked the Cumberland River. Gun crews stood at their cannons waiting for the big Federal ironclad boats that pummeled Fort Henry into submission to start their barrage on Fort Donelson. Soldiers that had managed to escape Fort Henry told him the Federal gunboats merely finished the job the surging river had started. Most of Fort Henry's forward cannons ended up underwater after the icy river invaded the low-lying fort. The latest report said that Fort Henry was now completely underwater. "Good!" many of Kyle's fellow Tennesseans said. It was one less place the Yankees could "plant their damned flag." Kyle supposed he was grateful for that.

He was anxious to get back to New Madrid. More importantly, he was anxious to check in on his home after reading his sister's letter over and over again. But with the Federals tightening their grip around Fort Donelson, Kyle feared he would never see his home again or the girl he loved.

He saw her just briefly when he first got home from Detroit. All those feelings from his childhood crush came crashing over him as she came down the stairs with his sister to greet him. He had been away for years, studying in the North. Perhaps, it was because his father knew of his feelings that he sent him far away, to prevent any unfortunate mistakes due to young and foolish love. Those years did nothing to quell the fire that Kyle felt for the now young woman who had grown into the complementing companion to his sister's beauty. He never got the chance to talk to her alone. He never got to do more than greet her politely in front of his parents and allow her to take his coat.

His father had been able to secure him a commission in one of the Tennessee volunteer regiments. Kyle was off to his unit the very next day after coming home. With little training or experience in leading men, Kyle's lieutenancy made him an aide to higher ranking officers. For the most part, he was a courier. That meant with the Federals cutting or either even spying on the telegraph lines, Kyle spent a lot of time on horseback carrying dispatches from one place to another.

He had been stationed at New Madrid running messages to the forts being built on either side of town, along the river, and even on the island they called "Number 10." It seemed like a funny name for an island to Kyle, but it was because it was the tenth island on the Mississippi, south of the Ohio River.

The island didn't seem that remarkable. It was a mile long and a quarter mile wide. Before the war, it was home to one man and his slaves. They grew corn, apples, and peaches there. But the island was immensely important to Kyle's commanders. That's because it sat in the first of two hairpin turns in the Mississippi River where the states of Missouri, Kentucky, and Tennessee all met. New Madrid sat on the second turn. Any Yankee ship trying to invade the South would have to slow down to navigate the waters between the island and the shore as it completed a tight 180° turn. Those ships would be easy pickings for artillery placed on the island. It was the perfect place to destroy Federal ships before they made their way to Memphis, Vicksburg, or even New Orleans. The Confederates also placed batteries at New Madrid and along the river to catch anything that made it past Island No. 10. It would be a gauntlet of fire and iron for any Yankee ship heading south on the Mississippi.

Losing the Mississippi would allow the Yankees to invade deep into the South. It would take away the Confederacy's own ability to move men and supplies quickly along the river. It would cut off western Confederate states like Texas, Louisiana, and Arkansas from the war. Most importantly, it would take away the farmers' ability to send their cotton to world markets through the Port of New Orleans, and that would mean financial ruin for the South.

The Mississippi had to be defended at all cost, but preparations at the vital double bend in the river were woefully behind schedule. This was due to a lack of supplies and men. That was the message Captain Gray, the man in charge of fortifying the island at the time, had sent Kyle to carry to General Sidney Johnston, Commander of all Confederate troops in the Western Theater. It took several days of hard riding to deliver those dispatches to Johnston at his headquarters, which was his room at the Covington Hotel in Bowling Green, Kentucky.

Johnston scoffed at the letter, "Everybody needs more men and supplies! I can't even defend our own position here! Fort Henry is lost and now the Yankees have the run of the Tennessee River. Gentlemen, we must consider withdrawing to Nashville and defending our supplies and rail lines there."

General Beauregard coughed and held his throat as he spoke softly, "If we fail to protect our rivers, the Yankees will win the West."

"What do you suggest?" Johnston turned to his second in command.

Beauregard grimaced as he cleared his throat, "Reinforce our position at Fort Donelson. We must prevent the ironclads from steaming up the Cumberland River and taking Nashville."

"You look terrible, Pierre," Johnston said to Beauregard, "are you able to lead the defense at Fort Donelson?"

"I'm afraid I feel worse than I look, Sidney," Beauregard replied. "Perhaps we should send Generals Floyd and Pillow with their troops to bolster Fort Donelson. I'll see to evacuating Columbus, as I'm afraid we are extended too far north in that position. Now that the Yankees have Fort Henry and the Tennessee River, we are cut off from the rest of our forces. I'll use the Columbus troops to fortify Island No. 10, New Madrid, and Fort Pillow along the Mississippi."

"Okay, let's get on the wires and let our commanders know what we expect of them. We'll start evacuating the troops here to Nashville," Johnston said. Kyle was trying to understand all that had been said and what was going on when General Johnston turned to him, "Lieutenant Bethune!"

"Uh…yes, sir!" Kyle stammered.

"Ready your horse. I'll have written dispatches for you to carry to General Pillow at Fort Defiance in Clarksville. You'll then put yourself at his disposal. We need him to take his men immediately downriver to Fort Donelson. If the Yankees get past there, there'll be no stopping them in Clarksville anyhow."

"Shouldn't I return to New Madrid?" Kyle asked, wanting to get closer to home so he could tend to the matter in his sister's letter. The officers in the room stared at him silently. Johnston lifted an eyebrow.

That put Kyle on another exhausting 60-mile ride southwest to Clarksville. From there, Pillow sent him 30 miles west to Fort Donelson with the wagon train full of supplies that couldn't be loaded onto the steamers that carried most of his troops. He got to Fort Donelson just in time to be boxed in by the approaching Federal troops. With nowhere to go, Kyle tried to finally get some sleep. That was interrupted by a cavalry boot nudging him awake.

"Get up, Daddy's Boy! It's time you earn that rank your papa bought you."

Kyle looked up to see a tall, gaunt man with glaring blue eyes and a thick goatee leering over him.

"Colonel Forrest…?" Kyle gaped.

"Ain't no time for sleeping, boy. It's time you did some real soldiering," Forrest growled. Kyle scrambled to his feet and stumbled along behind the terrifying cavalry leader to the stables where hundreds of men were saddling their horses and checking their guns.

"Gather around, boys," Forrest called out. The men immediately stopped what they were doing and circled around the fiery commander, many regarding him with unconcealed awe. "Them bluebellies are on their way, and if we let them, they'll trap us against the river and then shell us from the comfort of their trenches like the cowards they are. Are we gonna let 'em?!"

"No!" the men hollered.

"Y'God damn right! Saddle up, form a column, and follow me!" Forrest bellowed to the cheers of his men.

What have I gotten myself into… Kyle wondered.

They rode west along Ridge Road towards Fort Henry on the narrow strip of land between the Tennessee River and the Cumberland. If the Yankees were coming by land, this is where they'd meet them. Kyle rode behind Forrest and his brother. The Cavalry Colonel insisted he stay close to him. "I want to see you actually fight, Daddy's Boy," Forrest chided him, gaining a round of snickers from the nearby men.

They hadn't gone two miles when one of Forrest's forward scouts came back hurriedly down the trail. "Whoa," Forrest said softly, putting up his hand. The signal was repeated down the column, which came to a halt. With 500 men on horseback, the only sounds Kyle could hear were the occasional nicker of a horse or stamping of a hoof. Kyle checked to make sure his pistol was still on his hip. Then a quick look assured him that his saber and double-barreled shotgun were still in their saddle holsters as well.

The rider pulled up to Forrest and saluted. "Report," Forrest said.

"Yankee cavalry about a mile back, sir. They might be the van of a whole division," the rider told him.

Forrest glared up the trail, "What's the terrain like between us?"

The rider looked behind him and then returned his gaze to Forrest, "There's a clearing about a hundred yards up, then more woods."

"Perfect," Forrest said and then turned to his brother, "Jeff, dismount two companies and form a line just before the break in the woods. I want a mounted company on each side to guard the flanks. The rest will stay mounted at the ready in reserve," then to Kyle, "get your gun and follow me, Daddy's Boy, I'm gonna watch you kill your first man today." Kyle swallowed hard staring wide-eyed into Forrest's hard glare. Forrest's stern demeanor broke into a laugh, "Jesus, son, it ain't *that* bad!" The men nearby chuckled as well.

Kyle jumped off his horse and pulled the shotgun from its holster. The barrel had been shortened to 22 inches making it easier to draw from the saddle. One of Forrest's men snickered, "You think you're on a hunting trip with that thing?"

"I suppose I am," Kyle answered. The man looked down at his own rifled carbine and shrugged.

"Leave the saber with your horse," he said, stopping Kyle from buckling it to his hip, "it'll just get in your way, especially if we have to run back to the horses at the quick."

About 200 men made their way up the trail to the clearing. Kyle felt sure that any enemy within a mile would hear them as they trudged their way through. Forrest halted the men just before the break in the woods. With hand signals, he sent men along both sides of him to create a wall of fire just inside the wood line. Men found trees and logs to brace against, then saw to their weapons. Kyle helped move a fallen tree into place and then took cover behind it next to the Forrest brothers. He pulled the hammers back on his shotgun and placed percussion caps on the pins. He then checked his pistol to make sure each pin had a cap and each cylinder had a ball.

"No one shoot until I give the command," Forrest hissed.

Kyle stared hard into the tree line on the other side of the clearing. At first, he flinched at every sound or movement he detected, but then his eyes got heavy as the exhaustion from the last few days crept up on him.

"Here they come…" Jeff whispered. Kyle's eyes snapped open. He squinted at the wood line across the way. He saw nothing. Maybe the lieutenant was just nervous and seeing things, but then Kyle saw movement in the dark brush. Men on horses started to emerge from the trees. Kyle sucked in his breath as more and more came out of the darkness into the light that filled the clearing before him. They wore dark blue uniforms with brass buttons. Their kepi hats were pulled down so low that the shadows from their short visors extended half way down their noses revealing only beards and grim set mouths.

So many of them, Kyle thought. It was the first time he had seen Federal troops since he put on a Confederate uniform. Now he was supposed to kill them. Even worse, they were supposed to kill him. It didn't seem real. These were Americans. People he could have known in the time he spent in the North. *How is this possible…?*

One of the blue-clad men wearing a slouch hat pulled down low, put up a gloved hand causing the rest of the Federal horsemen to stop. *They see us,* Kyle thought, *They have to see us.*

"Hold…" Forrest whispered.

The man in the slouch hat motioned with his hand for the rest of them to straighten their line that spread out on either side of him. Once satisfied, he motioned with his hand forward.

"Steady…" Forrest growled.

My God, they are close! Kyle thought. It was maddening. Surely these Yankees could see the hundreds of men lying in the brush before them, but the sun was in their eyes and the Rebels were in the shade of the woods, so the Union soldiers kept approaching to the point that Kyle thought the Yankees would walk right over them.

"Fire!" Forrest roared. At first, a few carbines crackled, and then the whole line exploded in gunfire and smoke. Kyle pulled the first trigger of his shotgun. The kick and noise startled him. The smoke was so thick he couldn't see if he had hit anything. But he could hear the sounds of horses screaming and men yelling

"Fall back! It's an ambush! Fall back, God damn it!" he heard a voice in the smoke yell.

"Oh, God, I'm hit!" another voice shrieked.

"Keep firing! Let the fuckers have it!" Forrest yelled. The carbines were firing at a steady pace as the breech-loading Maynards didn't require all the steps and ramrodding the typical rifled musket needed.

Kyle fired his second barrel into the cloud of smoke where he heard the screaming Federals. He rolled over onto his back and reloaded both barrels through their smoking hot muzzles. He placed primers on the pins and rolled over onto his belly again to look for a target. Some of the smoke had cleared. He could see a horse on the ground screaming and thrashing its legs. Some of the Union soldiers were firing pistols towards the Confederate line as they turned their horses to ride back for cover. There were men on the ground screaming. Others were lying and aiming their guns back at the Rebels.

CRACK! FZZZZZZT! PING!

"What the hell was that!" Kyle blurted.

"They're firing at us, you idiot!" one of Forrest's men said, "Shoot!"

Kyle looked down the barrels of his gun, pointed them at the direction of any activity he saw and fired one and then fired the other barrel. Once again, the smoke didn't allow him to see if he had hit anything. He hoped it wasn't him that shot any of the horses.

They, too, lay screaming and dying, or dead in the field before him. Kyle reloaded. The Federals had finally formed into a line and started to return fire at a regular pace. Kyle wasn't sure if either line were doing much at all against the other up to that point, until he heard a man somewhere along his line yell, "Fuck, I'm hit!"

Just then a man scurried up to Forrest, crouching low with his head down. "Looks like the Yankees are forming up on our left, sir," he said

"Yeah, they think they're clever," Forrest spat, "Jeff!" he shouted to his brother, "hold the line here. We'll outflank their flanking maneuver before they get their act together. Daddy's Boy, to me!"

Kyle stopped himself from saying, "Me?" and got up into a crouch near Forrest.

"Come on, let's see how you ride," Forrest said, and with that, they were off running through the woods back to where the horses and the other men were. Forrest and Kyle approached a circle of Confederate captains. "Tommy, Dickie!" Forrest hailed two of them. "We got bluebellies forming up on our left. We'll hit them before they get a chance to organize. We go now. The rest of you be ready and keep an eye on the right. This might be a feint."

With that Forrest jumped on his horse and Kyle did the same. They rode along behind the Rebel line until they reached two lookouts on horseback. They saluted. "Report," Forrest said, returning the salute.

"Just about two hundred yards out. Not sure how many, maybe a whole regiment," one of the vedettes answered.

"Sabers out and form a line!" Forrest called. The horsemen spread out. The sound of steel sliding out of scabbards cut through the din of gunfire. Kyle pulled out his sword and looked to Forrest. "Advance!" Forrest called out.

At first, it was a walk, then a trot. As they came out of the woods, Kyle could see men in blue uniforms forming up in lines. "Charge!" Forrest bellowed. Kyle didn't even have to urge his horse forward. The animal followed the rest in an all-out gallop. The men in blue looked up in horror. Some fumbled with their rifles while trying to pull primers out of their pouches. Others dropped their guns and ran. Kyle raised his saber as they crashed into the mass of men and swung down indiscriminately into the chaotic crowd of screaming soldiers again and again. The blue-clad men scrambled in all directions; some fell right in front of him. He could feel their soft bodies break under the hooves of his horse.

They made it through the mass of men. Forrest twirled his sword around over his head to signal his men to turn around and then pointed his sword forward again. Forrest drove his men through the mass of blue troops once more. This time there were fewer of them. Some of the Federals fired their muskets in haste at the Rebel horsemen. Once back at the tree line, Forrest called his captains, "Form a line here. You are now protecting our flank. Kyle!"

It took Kyle a moment to realize Forrest meant him, "Yes, sir"

"Ride back to the fort. Tell General Buckner we need immediate reinforcements. We could be looking at a whole Yankee division here."

"Yes, sir!" Kyle said and then went to sheath his saber. It was then he realized it was covered in blood.

Kyle rode hard through the woods. He wasn't sure if the Minié balls whizzing past his head were real or imagined, but the constant crackle of muskets and the *…wait…! What was that…? A cannon…?* was certainly real. He waved his hat and called out to the forward pickets, "Don't shoot! Don't shoot! I'm friendly!" Wide-eyed men in rifle pits stared at him as he galloped past. General Simon Bolivar Buckner was already waiting for him when he entered the fort.

"What in tarnation is going on out there?!" asked the general before Kyle could even stop his horse or salute.

Kyle saluted, "Colonel Forrest is fully engaged with the enemy, sir, perhaps a whole division. The firefight is hot, sir. Colonel Forrest requests immediate support."

"Damn it all!" Buckner exploded, "General Pillow said no major engagements until he returns! You get back out there immediately and inform Colonel Forrest he is to withdraw his troops and return to the fort immediately!"

Kyle dashed back towards the sounds of battle. Leaving his horse with the rear vedette, he jogged in a half crouch to where Forrest was leading the fight from the front. "Sir, General Buckner insists we withdraw a immediately. He says we are not to provoke any major engagements until General Pillow returns," Kyle told him.

Forrest spat on the ground, "Those damned fools can't make a decision to save their lives. We could lick them right here before they get a chance to dig in." Forrest let out a long breath, "Well, all right then…"

The withdrawal was orderly. Forrest left two companies to hold the Federals down while the rest of the men were able to mount and ride back to the fort. Then his two remaining companies took turns covering each other as they made their way back. Kyle tried hard to hide his relief at being done with the fight for the day.

The Confederates spent the next day working on their earthworks as Federal sharpshooters picked off any man foolish enough to offer a target. Forrest dragged Kyle out again with a detachment of his men to silence them.

"All right, Daddy's Boy, you see that fool of a Yankee up in that tree down yonder?" Forrest asked, pointing out past the Rebel line.

Kyle squinted. He could see a blurry, blue smear in the leafless tree that he assumed was a Federal soldier. He seemed to be about 600 yards away.

"…Uh huh…" Kyle offered.

"He's been murdering our boys all day while they've been trying to build our defenses," Forrest gritted through his teeth, as he looked towards the sharpshooter with unbridled hatred. Then he smiled and turned to Kyle, "Kill him."

Kyle squinted at the blue blur again and then pulled his shotgun to his shoulder. Forrest turned and grinned at his men. A low chuckle rippled among them. Kyle lined his eye along the two short barrels and sighted the blue blur in the tree. He let out his breath and pulled the trigger.

BAM!

Birds flew off, squawking in protest. The smoke cleared to reveal the blue blur was still in the tree. The men cackled with laughter.

"Son, you can't hit anything with that short-barreled shotgun unless it's ten feet in front of you," Forrest chuckled. "Jonesy! Give me your Maynard!" One of his troopers handed him a carbine rifle. It was a funny looking weapon to Kyle. It too had a short barrel but with no forestock. Forrest pushed a lever that covered the trigger forward to crack open the breech near the shoulder stock. He checked to see that it was loaded. He snapped the barrel shut, pulled the hammer back, and placed a percussion cap on the nipple. Forrest spat on the ground and then sighted the gun.

CRACK!

Kyle held his breath for a moment, staring at the blue blur in the tree. Just as he was trying to decide how to respond to the terrifying leader missing the shot, the blur slowly leaned to one side, and then fell out of the tree like a discarded rag doll.

"Woo-wee!" yelled one of the men. The rest broke into cheers. Even the artillery boys nearby were throwing their hats into the air. Forrest handed the carbine back to Jonesy while eyeing Kyle hard. He then spat on the ground and walked away.

It snowed that night, leaving several inches on the ground. It was Valentine's Day and Kyle read the letter again, and even though it was from his sister's hand, he could sense the distress of the girl he loved behind it. Elijah, the kind boy that cared for the horses with a sense of duty that Kyle could only describe as noble, had run away. Rumor had it that he had been captured and pressed into labor at fortifications at New Madrid. Liza was heartsick with worry and grief. Kyle's sister, Kathryn, pleaded with him, asking if there anything he could do? Kyle shuddered with cold and frustration. He was so far away from being able to help, so far from home, so far from…her.

Kyle's thoughts drifted back to Liza, her large brown eyes, sumptuous lips, dark smooth skin, and excruciatingly curved body. Kyle began to feel the embarrassment of his arousal tightening his pants, giving him a sense of warmth in the bitter cold.

"Here they come!" someone shouted.

Kyle snapped out of his reverie and looked up at the river. Ugly black smoke billowed from behind the bend, and then the first of them began to appear: low-lying black metal monsters rounded the bend. The Federal ironclads were here in force to pound Fort Donelson into submission.

Chapter Six: The Escape

"Parson, for God's sake, pray! Nothing but almighty God can save this fort now!"

Kyle turned to see Colonel Forrest speaking to a terrified looking Major Kelly. Kelly had been a preacher before the war. Now he stood amongst the officers who came out to watch the approaching doom from the parapets of the upper battery. Kyle turned back to the river. Four black ironclad steamers lined side-by-side across the river were making their way upstream to the fort, behind them a pair of wooden gunboats followed.

BOOM! THHHHHHHHHHP!

Every man in Kyle's periphery ducked as the bow of one of the ships erupted in fire and smoke. A shell whistled over their heads and exploded in the camp behind them. Confederate gun crews scrambled around their cannons, ramming, charging, and aiming them.

BOOM!

The first of the Rebel lanyards was pulled by a sergeant. Soon the Confederate batteries were firing in full force. The air smelled of rotten eggs as smoke wisped around the parapets. The air seemed alive with hot shell and shot as the Federal boats returned fire, but the dread Kyle and those around him were feeling began to dissipate. The Federals were firing up at the fort that sat on a bluff high above the river. That caused most of their shells to pass harmlessly over the heads of the Confederates, but the Confederates were able to pour plunging fire into the enemy below, and they were beginning to hit their targets.

"Now boys, see me take chimney," shouted one of the Rebel gunmen, as he pulled the lanyard of his 32-pounder.

BOOM!

Down went a smokestack on one of the ships. The enormous metal beast sputtered, faltered, and then fell behind the others, drifting harmlessly back down the river from where it came. A cheer broke out amongst the Confederates. The young man who made the shot called out again to the enemy ships below, "Come on, you cowardly scoundrels! You are not at Fort Henry!"

The Confederates continued to pour fire on the Federal gunboats until one by one the big metal ships became disabled and floated back downstream. The men cheered loudly as the last of them dropped out of the fight. The big, Federal ships that took Fort Henry, had failed at Fort Donelson.

The cheer felt among the men did not carry into the war council that evening. Kyle sat just outside the room at the Dover Hotel where General Floyd made his headquarters. Kyle was waiting to carry orders to field commanders at a moment's notice. He couldn't help but hear the generals arguing inside.

"I tell you, repelling the gunboats today was a mere distraction," General Buckner declared to the room. "Every minute, Grant reinforces and tightens his grip around us. We must break out and save our army before the trap is sealed!"

"Bah! The only thing that useless drunk has ever been able to trap is a bottle of whiskey," General Pillow retorted.

"Sir, you would do well not to insult my friend in my presence, nor underestimate him," Buckner replied. "True, Ulysses does not idle well, but I studied with him at West Point, and served with him in Mexico, put to a task, there's no stopping that man."

"Your friend?" Pillow cocked an eyebrow, "Just whose side are you on?"

"Sir!" Buckner leaped from his chair in anger.

"Enough!" General Floyd bellowed. "Easy…we are all on the same side here, gentlemen," Floyd placed a hand on Buckner's shoulder, "and bickering isn't going to dig us out of this hole. I'm afraid General Buckner is right."

Pillow let out a sigh.

"Furthermore," Floyd continued after pausing to stare Pillow into submission, "my orders from General Johnston are to hold the Federals here as long as we can, but we must abandon the fort and save our army as the odds turn against us. We must find a way to break out and join General Johnston's forces at Nashville."

Buckner spoke next, "Colonel Forrest reports that the enemy's right flank does not extend all the way to the river. He thinks those troops could be rolled back, thus opening the Wynn's Ferry Road to our purpose."

"General Pillow," Floyd turned to his other brigade commander, "can your men be ready to lead the attack?"

"Certainly!" Pillow blustered, "We can beat the enemy back and more. We can crush them and hold the fort indefinitely."

Floyd scowled, placing his hands on his hips.

"...or leave at our leisure," Pillow finished.

"It will be no leisurely affair, gentlemen," Floyd said. "Be ready to move at 4am. You will push the enemy back on his right and open the way to Wynn's Ferry Road. Once you've opened the door, General Buckner will hold it, pinning the enemy down west of the road as we evacuate. He will then form the rear guard as we make our way to Nashville. Colonel Forrest's cavalry will protect our flanks as we march. Lieutenant Bethune!"

Kyle scrambled to his feet and popped his head into the room, "Sir?"

"Don't pretend you weren't listening, son, we don't have time. I have orders for you to carry to our commanders," Floyd said, and then to the room, "gentlemen, in a few hours we fight our way out. Make your men ready."

The next several hours were a flurry of activity as snow began to fall on the Rebel troops preparing for battle. Then an odd silence fell among the men in the early morning as they stood ready. Kyle watched the cold breath roll out of his horse. Snowflakes landed softly between the animal's ears. The horse nickered and shook its head to dust the snow off. Kyle then heard a whistle in the distance. Next was sound of metal scraping against metal as Forrest pulled his saber from its scabbard and pointed it forward, "That's the signal, boys. Move out."

Kyle rode along with Forrest's command. They were the Confederates' far left flank. The first crackle of muskets popped off as Union pickets started to respond to the oncoming line of Rebel soldiers. The Union men placed out in front of their lines to watch for such an attack, were stunned at the sight of the enormous Confederate force descending upon their positions. Kyle saw a white-faced, opened-mouth Yankee scramble to fire off a wild shot before dashing back to the main Federal line, certainly to warn the rest.

Soon the Union troops began to organize into their own lines only to offer a volley of musket fire before falling back. It was working. The Rebel forces were pushing the Yankees back before they even had a chance to mount any serious resistance. The Southern boys pushed on with glee as they were soon tramping across ground that had been just recently occupied by the blue-clad soldiers. It wasn't until the Confederates had pushed the Federals well off the Wynn's Ferry Road that a well-fortified Yankee line stopped the advance. Still, the escape route was open. All they had to do was take it.

Not content with merely protecting the left flank, Forrest's troops were busy taking prisoners and capturing Union guns. Kyle rode with Forrest as he and a small detachment overwhelmed a Federal gun crew who were trying to turn their cannon as quickly as possible on the overwhelming Rebels. Forrest rode his horse into the crew of 10 men, leveling his pistol at one of the soldiers. That soldier immediately put his hands up and quivered under the glare of the terrifying horsemen.

"Make one damn move and I kill all of you right now," Forrest growled, but then lifted his eyes from his captives to stare at the Confederate troops walking back towards the fort en masse. "What in God's name are they doing…?" he said to no one. "Jonesy!" he barked at one of his men.

"Yes, sir!" the trooper answered.

"Ride out there find out why they're retreating."

"Yes, sir!" the trooper answered and then spurred his horse towards the retreating Confederates. Moments later he returned. "Sir, the men I spoke to say that General Pillow ordered his men back to the fort now that the Yankees are licked."

"Licked?!" Forrest spat, "God damn it, that was not the plan!" Forrest stood up in his stirrups trying to get a better view of what was going on around him. Then, with a sigh, slumped back into his saddle, "Alright, tell the men to fall back to the fort, otherwise we'll be cut off from the rest." And with that, the Confederate troops gave the ground they had won, back to the Union.

"In the name of God, General Pillow," General Floyd glared at his subordinate officer, "what have we've been fighting for all day?! Certainly not to show our powers…but solely to secure the Wynn's Ferry Road…and after securing it…you order it given up?!"

"Sir," Pillow offered, "the Yankees are soundly whipped. We can leave at our leisure."

Kyle sat outside the meeting room at the Dover Hotel once again, listening to commanders argue. Floyd let out a sigh, "Our scouts say they've spotted enemy campfires all across the road. They have retaken it!"

General Buckner spoke next, "General Grant is closing the hole we created with reinforcements as we speak. Gentlemen, our only choice is to surrender the fort before we sacrifice any more precious lives on a useless attempt to hold it, or break free."

"I cannot surrender," Floyd said softly, "there is a price on my head for my actions during my last days as Secretary of War for the United States. They will hang me as a traitor for sure. General Pillow, I turn the command over to you, Sir."

General Pillow looked around the room with his mouth agape in fear. "…And I pass it!" he said turning to General Buckner.

Buckner let out a deep and long sigh, "I assume it. I'll start writing a letter asking for terms for our capitulation."

Kyle was stunned by what he heard. Just then Colonel Forrest came storming past him, spitting on the floor before barging into the room.

"I did not come here with the purpose of surrendering my command," Forrest snarled at the surprised Generals, "and would not do it if they would follow me out. I intend to go out if I save but one man!"

Pillow looked around the room nervously, "I think Colonel Forrest should be allowed to try to save his troops if he can."

Buckner was the only man able to not look away from Forrest's glare. He paused for a moment and then said, "Fine, but you must remove your men before I ask for terms."

Forrest then looked back to Pillow, "What should I do?"

"Cut your way out," Pillow respond.

"By God, I will!" Forrest declared and then turned on his heel and stormed out of the room. He stopped to give Kyle a look before leaving, "It's your choice, son, you can spend the rest of your life in a federal prison, or you can come with me, but you better come now." Kyle stood for a moment. He wondered who was in charge now if anyone! Surrendering to the Yankees with General Buckner certainly wouldn't get him any closer to home, so he shrugged his shoulders and jogged off to catch up with the stormy cavalry leader.

By four in the morning, they were ready to make their break. Forrest mustered all the men he could to go with him, including non-cavalry men who took horses that were meant for moving carts and cannon for their rides. There were about 500 men in all willing to make the run. They headed east on the Old Charlotte Road. It wasn't long until three scouts came galloping back. "Report," Forrest, said returning their salute.

"Sir!" one of the scouts replied breathlessly, "We've seen Union troops lined along the side of the road!"

"Along the side of the road?" Forrest wondered out loud, why they weren't blocking the road outright? "Jeffy, Kyle…to me! I want to see for myself. The rest of you wait here and be ready for anything."

The three rode out in the early morning gloom. Kyle could see them, hundreds of silhouettes lining the road, seemingly shoulder to shoulder. "Wait a minute…" Forrest mumbled in annoyance. Kyle was stunned at how cavalier Forrest seemed as he approached the silent line of figures along the road. Then he realized the line was both silent and still. Forrest kicked a post, "It's a God damn picket fence, the fools!" Kyle let out a slightly nervous chuckle, mostly in relief. "But what do we have here?" Forrest said looking at the glow of what seemed to be a nearby campfire just inside the wood line. He pulled out his pistol and urged his horse forward. Kyle and Jeff Forrest followed cautiously.

The light of the fire revealed two men in blue uniforms lying next to it. One stared up at nothing as he shivered feverishly. The other lay there with his ruined leg stretched out. He had his hands up as they approached. Forrest held his revolver on him.

"Don't shoot, sir. We're injured!" the man said.

"Where's the rest of your unit?" Forrest asked.

"I don't know, sir," the man said, "we can't walk. I'm just trying to keep him alive until we're rescued… or captured."

"What troop movements have you seen overnight?" Forrest asked.

"Just scouts, sir, we couldn't tell if they were ours or yours," the man said. Forrest regarded them for a moment longer and then turned his horse back towards his own troops. "Sir!" the injured man called out, "do you have any food you can spare?"

"There's probably plenty of food where you came from! Go home, Billy Yank!" Forrest growled as he started riding off. He stopped. "God damn it…" he hissed. He reached into his haversack and pulled out two pieces of hardtack. "Go give them these," as he handed them to his brother.

Daylight spread across the snow-covered ground as they approached Lick Creek which was swollen from the recent rains. Its swirling black water had swallowed the road. Ice formed along its banks. Kyle could see dead branches passing by hurriedly with the current. "Alright, I need someone to go test the depth to see if it's still passable," Forrest said. No one answered. "God damn it," Forrest mumbled, as he spurred his horse into the icy water. Men held their breath as the water got as high as his saddle skirt, but then their leader passed the center, and soon the horse's legs were splashing the water as it hurried to get out on the other side. "Alright then," Forrest called out to the men on the other side, "let's go!"

Kyle was among the company of men placed to cover the crossing. They scanned the other side of the creek, searching for any signs of the enemy as hundreds of men and horses made their way across.

Once everyone got to the other side, Kyle was selected with three other men to watch for an enemy crossing while the rest of the men made their way to Nashville. "Wait here for another hour," Lieutenant Jeff Forrest told them, "if you don't see nothing, catch up to the rest of us."

The four of them didn't talk much as they waited. Kyle diligently watched the other side, waiting to see a mass of blue-uniformed men. They never came. He could hear the soft snoring of one of the men who had dozed off in his saddle. The sun rose higher, glistening off the water. Kyle was feeling his eyelids getting heavier when one of the men broke the silence.

"That's about an hour, boys, we should go," he said snapping his pocket watch shut.

CRACK!

The sound of a rifle broke the peace of the morning, and just like that, the man with the watch was dead on the ground. His horse ran off in panic. Kyle turned to see a squad of Union men galloping towards them. They were racing along the same side of the creek as Kyle's vedette. They had their pistols out and were firing.

"Run!" yelled one of the Rebels. Kyle spurred his horse as the three ran in the same direction the rest of their troops had taken an hour before.

CRACK! THUNK!

Kyle felt the impact of the bullet but couldn't tell where he was hit. He frantically patted himself trying to find the wound as his horse sped down the road. He found no sign of blood on himself. The horse slowed from a gallop to a trot, and then an amble. "Oh, no…" Kyle moaned. "Oh, my sweet boy…" Kyle patted his horse's neck. The horse let out an appreciative snort and then buckled, falling to the knees on its forelimbs. "Oh, please, no…" Kyle whimpered. The squad of Federal horsemen raced by. Kyle's horse fell over to its side with a thud, pinning Kyle's leg to the ground. "Oh, my sweet friend…" Kyle said and then let out a sob.

He could hear the clomp of a horse returning to where he was pinned. A man in blue walked into his field of vision with his revolver trained on Kyle. "Well, well, well," the man sneered, "what do we have here? A Rebel rat caught in a trap." Kyle glared at him with tear-blurred eyes.

"You killed my horse, you fucking animal!" Kyle screeched at him. He thrashed about trying to free his pistol from its holster, but it was pinned under his thigh held down by the weight of the horse.

The man laughed as he holstered his own. "Now, I got to figure out what to do with you," he said, looking off in the direction of his friends who had continued their pursuit of the other Rebels. Kyle reached out for the double barrel shotgun still in its saddle holster. The man turned, realized the danger, and fumbled to pull his own pistol back from its holster. Kyle pulled the hammer back and fired the gun with a scream. The force of the gun threw his arm back, tossing the weapon out of reach behind him. The man dropped his own gun and clutched his ruined face with both hands. He dropped to the ground on the other side of the horse screaming and thrashing in agony. Kyle lay there listening to the man die for what seemed to be an eternity. The screams turned to gurgling, coughs, labored breathing, and then finally, merciful silence.

Kyle lay there staring at the sky. He wanted to sleep. He felt himself drifting off. He suddenly snapped awake. *If I stay here, I will die*, he thought. He worked at wiggling his numb leg free from the dead horse. Pressing his other foot against the saddle, he was eventually able to create enough leverage to pull himself free.

He lay there sure that his leg was broken. He couldn't feel a thing, but then a tingling sensation came. He sat up and felt his leg. There were no apparent injuries. He used his arms to bend his knee back and forth. Slowly, the feeling in his seemingly dead leg returned. Soon he was able to get up to his feet.

The scene before him was ghastly. His horse and the Union trooper lay in a puddle of shared blood. The man lay in a sprawled position that portrayed the agony of his last moments, his hands still clutching his caved in face. Kyle nudged him with his foot: no response. He reached down and pulled the revolver from the man's holster and tucked it into his belt. A horse nickered behind him. Kyle spun around drawing the pistol. The man's horse was tied to a tree. It pawed the ground as Kyle approached. There was food in the saddle bag: salt pork, hardtack, a bag of coffee, brown sugar, even a bottle of whiskey. He ate some of the pork as he soaked the hardtack in the tin cup he found in the bag with a little whiskey and sugar to soften it. He fingered the mush into his mouth and washed it down with a hard pull from the whiskey. It seemed like the best meal he had had in weeks.

He let out a sigh. He was alone. He looked to the east where Forrest had led his cavalry towards Nashville. The men he had been separated from went that way too, chased by the Federal cavalry squad. He looked west, no sounds of battle which probably meant the fort had been surrendered. He thought it over as he transferred his things to the new horse. He mounted the animal, which didn't seem to mind the new rider. He looked east and west again, and then made up his mind. He was going home.

Crowds lined the streets of St. Louis to cheer the Federal troops as they marched out of the Benton Barracks and made their way to the transports moored at the river. The men in blue were excited to be done with their training and off to see some real action. They called it "seeing the elephant" which meant actually fighting in a real battle. They revered men that had been through the trials of combat and regaled their tales. Men would listen wide-eyed, each imagining himself doing heroic deeds as bombs burst and bullets whizzed around him.

Carl rode Bess in formation with the other brown horses of Company H. This day could not have come soon enough for him either. The early excitement of training at the Benton Barracks had soon turned into tedium. The army base started to seem more and more like a prison during the cold months he spent there. Then he got sick, like hundreds of other men. A fever put him in the hospital along with others who suffered the same ailment, as well as dysentery and various other maladies that covered sick men's faces with spots and bumps. The hospital smelled of urine, vomit, and feces. Carl felt the longer he stayed there, the more likely he would die. Many did. A bed that held a man moaning in feverish dreams the night before would be empty the next day. Many men died without ever seeing the enemy. Some lucky ones were sent home. Carl merely got better and then returned to duty which consisted of riding, shooting, hacking straw dummies, and cleaning, lots of cleaning. So to be out of the Benton Barracks with its drilling, bugs, and sickness was a good thing to Carl, regardless of looming threat of real battle.

After loading their horses below, the men found spots where they could on the steamboat "Empress." The boys of Company H clustered around their captain who told them what he could about their upcoming mission. "We should get to Commerce by the morning, so sleep well, boys. It might be your last chance," Captain Newman said with his usual ornery smile. They were to disembark there and then march towards New Madrid where the Rebels had dug in. "There's a double bend in the river," Newman drew an imaginary sideways "S" on the floor with his finger, "where the Rebels have decided to make their stand. If we clear them out of the island in the first bend here, and the town of New Madrid here in the second bend, we'll have the rule of the river all the way down to Fort Pillow and maybe even Memphis." Men peered over each other's shoulders to look at the imaginary map he was drawing on the floor.

"Now our navy boys will take out the batteries on the island, Island Number 10, as it is called," he continued, "we'll handle taking the town, but first we have to march through 45 miles of swampland to get there."

"Isn't that swamp filled with Jeff Thompson's Swamp Rats, sir?" Chucky asked.

"Yeah, but they're nothing more than a bunch of toothless butt-fuckers," Newman grinned, causing a rupture of laughs from men. "Trust me, boys. You are professionally trained soldiers. We out man them, we out gun them, and we have all our teeth." Newman scanned the room of laughing men noting the gaps in some of their mouths, "Well, at least most of us do." The men continued to chuckle, ribbing the ones unfortunate enough to have missing teeth.

The men were in good spirits and spent most of the night talking and laughing instead of taking the advice about getting a good night's sleep. Much of the conversation was about Jeff Thompson and his Swamp Rats. Some said they were a group of partisan raiders that harassed Federal supply lines from St. Louis to Memphis. Others said he was in command of a full Confederate cavalry force that was unstoppable. Men bragged about what they were going to do when they met "Ol' Jeff Thompson." Carl tried his best to ignore them and sleep.

Fog covered the landing site at the village of Commerce making unloading onto the narrow wharf difficult. Constant rains swelled the river and flooded the nearby area turning the roads into rivers of mud. The 2nd Michigan Cavalry moved out dividing their force into three battalions, each taking a separate route. Carl's battalion put a platoon of horsemen out about a hundred feet from the main group as a forward guard. They tried to do the same on each side to protect their flanks and rear, but the muddy ground and heavy brush made parade ground formations nearly impossible, so for the most part, they were an unorganized mass of men on horses plodding through the mud.

Men scanned the woods, wide-eyed in search of Jeff Thompson and his ghostly men. Every owl call, every deer that scampered off caused an immediate hair-raising dread among the men. The rain came back at nightfall. Carl's group failed to reach the designated meeting spot with the other battalions, so they waited for daylight to come before continuing. Men looked for fallen logs to perch on and tried to sleep a bit as their horses stood in knee-deep water. Once morning came they were able to find the camp where the rest of the troops had spent the night. Coffee, breakfast, and a brief rest awaited them before they headed out again.

Since they had gotten bogged down in the swamp the day before, Carl's battalion was put in the lead as they made their way to Sikeston, which was the next waypoint along their path to New Madrid. The other two battalions made up the rear flanks. This made for a much easier ride as it put them on road. Even though it was muddy, it was better than trudging through the swamp like the day before.

Much of the apprehension for Jeff Thompson and his marauding Swamp Rats had dissipated in the cold rain and hungry march. Men thought more about when the next hot meal would come than they worried about murderous Rebels attacking them out of nowhere.

Carl's mind had numbed to the rhythm of the ride. He was in the vanguard, meaning his squad of men were out in front of the main body of troops to detect any problems along the road. They had plenty, mostly from felled trees along the way blocking their path. Bridges had been burned too. "The work of the Swamp Rats for sure," the men would mumble. Each time they would have to halt the advance while the engineers went to work clearing the way or fixing the crossings.

It was a slow go for sure. That's why Carl was surprised to see three cannons set up ahead in the road. "How did our artillery get ahead of us?" Carl asked to no one in particular around him.

BOOM! FFFFFFFFT! BAM!

One of the pieces exploded in smoke and fire.
"Holy shit! They're firing at us!" Carl yelled.
"Get down, you damn fools! It's the enemy!" Sergeant Barth shouted. The small squad of horsemen quickly dismounted, pulling their Colt revolving rifles from their holsters. Two of the soldiers walked the horses back to a place where they could be tied up and out of the way. A third galloped back to the main force to inform them of the newly found peril. Carl found a place along the road to lie down and point his carbine towards the enemy cannons. The wet grass immediately soaked his uniform.

CRACK!

Chucky fired off a shot. Then someone else did nearby. Soon everyone around Carl was firing as rapidly as they could. Men emptied all six cylinders of their revolving carbines, reloaded, and fired again. Carl looked down at his gun, still cold in his hands, and then back towards the Rebel cannons. For as much lead as they were throwing down the road, Carl couldn't see if anybody was actually hitting anything. The three Rebel artillery pieces continued to fire back as well, but the shots were high. Carl could hear them screaming overhead and thumping into the ground behind him. Soon more men took up positions around him as the rest of the battalion caught up. Some looked scared out of their wits. Others were eager to finally fire at their first found enemies of the war. At this point, he figured he ought to be shooting too, but it seemed so weird to be actually shooting at people. He shrugged and brought his carbine to his shoulder, looking for something to shoot at.

"Cease fire! Cease fire!" the command came, and then was repeated down the line. Carl let out a sigh and lowered his gun. He looked back towards the yelling officers and sergeants to see why they were ordering the ceasefire. Then he heard a rumbling that brought his attention back forward. Across his field of vision came a detachment of Union horseman from the left bearing down on the enemy gunmen's flank. The Rebels had no time to turn their cannons or to form a line to meet the charging Federals. So the ones that could, took to their horses and ran. Others threw their hands in the air as members of the 7th Indiana Cavalry were quickly upon them with their guns and sabers out.

After a while, Carl's battalion was called forward. They rode past the three artillery pieces. They were small caliber guns, now in possession of the US Army. Carl caught a glimpse of some of the Rebel soldiers that had been captured. It amazed him to actually see them up close. Some of them were in uniforms that made them looked like officers, others were wearing plain civilian clothing. Carl, for a moment, wondered if any of them were Kyle, but then chided himself for being foolish. *What are the chances of that?* he thought to himself. Still, he was dying to ask them if they knew Kyle Bethune or if was he okay? Could he visit him? But he knew he was being naive. It was a big war in a big country. What were the chances?

Federal officers were questioning the prisoners as he rode by. By the time Carl's battalion made it to Sikeston, the fruit of that questioning had been leaked and spread among the men quickly. According to the prisoners, the Rebels had 10,000 infantry, 900 cavalry, and four batteries of field artillery. Those numbers filled some men with dread, others with glee. "We can lick 'em for sure, boys!" Carl could hear men boasting around the campfires as they ate their evening meal.

Carl and his fellow troops spent a few days in Sikeston as the Federal forces consolidated before their push into New Madrid. Every day more cannons arrived by rail. Other than looking to their horses and equipment or pulling vedette duty, there was plenty of free time. Many caught up on their letter writing. Some found the one tavern in town to spend what little money they had on them. The owner was openly a supporter of the secessionist cause but didn't mind taking Federal money from the boys in blue who tolerated his pro-Confederate quips so long as he kept pouring the whiskey.

Mail had come in with one of the shipments of supplies. Carl was excited to get a letter from Francis, who was the only one who bothered to write to him. Francis said that Anna sends her love, but her family had forbidden her to write to him. He was both relieved and disappointed by that. Still, the picture in his locket was at times, his greatest source of comfort. His mom was well too, but melancholy as always. There was talk about forming a colored infantry unit and Francis hoped that his education and social standing would garner him a high rank. "Maybe I'll even outrank you!" he wrote with a smiley face. *The fool,* Carl thought. *No one in their right mind should sign up for this if they have a choice.* He would write to discourage him at the first opportunity. He had vedette duty that afternoon and letter writing, or doing anything other than sitting on a horse scanning the horizon for enemy activity was frowned upon.

Carl's squad geared up and rode out on the road that ran straight south from Sikeston to New Madrid. They didn't have to go far to find the vedette already there that they were relieving. Those men had been out there all morning watching the road from their saddles.

"See anything interesting?" Sergeant Barth called out to them.

"We seen a few men on horseback appear out yonder come out the woods," the leader of the morning vedette pointed down the road, "but they took one look at us and headed back…probably about an hour ago."

The morning crew rode back to town, eager to get a meal as Carl and his squad settled in for what they expected to be a long boring afternoon of staring down the road. Carl snatched another look at Anna in his locket and felt a bit of an arousal stirring in his pants. *Maybe I can find some privacy at some point…*he was thinking when Sergeant Barth's voice brought him back to reality.

"What's going on here…?"

Carl squinted down the road. Horsemen started coming out of the woods and gathering on the road before them. They looked back at Carl and his group using their hands as visors. One of them had field glasses. He set them down and started signaling to someone in the woods to come out. A team of horses emerged pulling a cannon.

"Bates!" Barth shouted.

"Yes, Sergeant!" the private responded nudging his horse closer to Sergeant Barth.

"Ride back to town and tell them we've got enemy field artillery and cavalry forming up about a half mile from our position. Looks like six guns and a company of horsemen. We'll hold the road here," Barth ordered.

"Yes, Sergeant!" Bates turned and spurred his horse, "Hah!" he cried, as he sped off towards town. Carl looked back at the enemy before him. He hoped help would come soon because surely their squad couldn't take on what looked like to be about a hundred men on horseback and a battery of cannon.

Once the Rebels set up their cannons on either side of the road, they unfurled a large regimental flag.

"Who the hell are these guys...?" Chucky pondered out loud.

"I don't know, but they think rather highly of themselves," Sergeant Barth responded.

After what looked like a conference around their flag, one of the officers broke away from the group and trotted towards the Federals. The feather in his hat bounced with the horse's gait. Chucky raised his carbine. Sergeant Barth put his hand on the barrel and gently pushed it down, "Easy, lad. I think this peacock wants to talk," and then with his hand cuffed around his mouth he shouted towards the approaching horseman, "whose men are you?!"

The man reigned his horse to a stop about 80 yards from the nervous Federals. He smiled and then with a grandiose gesture with his hand he guided their gaze back to the Rebel force that was formed up on the road behind him.

"Why, General Jeff Thompson's, sir!"

"There's your swamp rats, boys..." Barth mumbled to his men. "What are you doing here?!" he called back to the man.

"Hunting for a fight!" the man called back.

Sergeant Barth heard the clomp of horses coming from behind him, then saw a large group of blue-clad horsemen swinging wide into a flanking position on the right. "By God, you'll get one!" Barth shouted back. The smile on the Rebel officer's face dropped as he realized they were now facing a much larger force than they had assumed. He grabbed his hat as he turned his horse and broke into a full gallop back to the Rebel line.

The men there started scrambling as they realized they were suddenly outgunned and outflanked. Only a few got off a shot or managed to pull the lanyard on one of the cannons before breaking into an all out-run.

"Come on, boys!" Barth called, "This is what we signed up for!" The chase was on. Soon Carl's vedette was absorbed by a mass of Illinois Cavalry men that came to relieve them. Hundreds of them barreled down the road after the fleeing Rebels. Sometimes even getting close enough to fire off a pistol shot.

The Rebels started breaking off into smaller groups darting into the tree line on either side of the road. Carl's vedette followed one group into the woods, thundering down dark forest trails, popping off shots at each other. The groups splintered even further. Groups of four split into twos, and then even lone Confederates picking their own forks in the trails causing the Federal pursuers to separate as well, as they wound their way through twisting forest paths.

Carl began to worry. His group had gotten smaller and smaller until he was all by himself chasing a soldier he hadn't seen in the last 20 minutes. *Where am I?* he wondered as he looked around the dark woods that surrounded him. At this point, he wasn't sure how far he had gone, *10, 15 miles? More?* It seemed like he had been gone way too long. He could tell that night was approaching, diminishing his chances of finding his way back to his comrades before dark. He worried that he might now have bumbled his way into enemy territory. *What am I going to do?* he wondered.

He decided to keep moving. At this point, he wasn't even sure which direction he had come from or which direction the enemy was. He stopped again. He looked around him, trying to get his bearing in the woods. The sun was now far too low for a city boy like him to know which direction it was setting. That's when he saw him, like a ghost in the corner of his eye. A Confederate soldier on a horse was watching him carefully, but he didn't look like the others. Carl turned and caught a glimpse of him before the man dashed off. But Carl could see this man was much more ragged and dirtier than the others he had been chasing. His uniform was filthy and in tatters. He wore a scraggly blond beard that hid most of his face. Carl got a flash of the man's hard, blue eyes just before he disappeared like the apparition he seemed to be.

"Wait!" Carl called and rode off after him.

They raced deeper into the woods. Carl would catch glimpses of the man before he'd disappear around another bend in the heavy brush. Soon the trail seemed to grow cold again. Carl walked his horse cautiously through the darkening woods thinking he was now more lost than ever.

The nicker of a horse caused him to pull out his pistol. He stopped briefly, looked around, then prodded his horse forward. Under the dark canopy of trees, he saw a horse. He pointed his pistol at it, then realized there was no rider. The horse just looked at him mildly. Its reigns were tied to a tree.

WHOMP!

Something large and heavy fell upon him from above, and down he went. He was now wrestling with a man on the forest floor. The man was trying to strangle him. Carl broke the hold and scampered to his feet. He reached for his pistol in his holster. It was gone. He realized it must have been knocked out of his hand when he went down. He pulled his saber from his horse saddle. The man got up and did the same.

After a brief pause, the bearded Rebel charged him with his saber held high. Carl could see the rage in the man's steely, blue eyes. The stranger brought his saber down on Carl's head. Carl blocked it, but the man kicked out Carl's front foot, causing him to tumble to the ground once again. The man stepped on Carl's sword arm and pressed the tip of his saber into Carl's neck.

Carl looked up at the glaring blue eyes that seemed to be the only thing reflecting the fading light on the bearded face. "Surrender, you Yankee Bastard," the man gritted through his teeth.

Carl paused, "Wait a minute…" the fear washing out of him. It was replaced by an incredulous astonishment, "…Kyle?"

The man's hard, blue eyes sharpened and then softened as all the rage emptied out of them. The saber point pulled away from Carl's neck and the foot came off his arm.

"Carl…?" Kyle gasped, and then dropped to his knee throwing his saber to the ground, "My God, are you hurt?!"

"I'm fine, just a little winded. I think you got the better of me," Carl said, sitting up with the help of his friend. "How is this possible?"

Kyle looked around quickly, suddenly aware of his surroundings, "Are there many more of you?"

"There was, but I got separated chasing down your boys," Carl said.

"My boys?" Kyle asked.

"Weren't you with Jeff Thompson's troops?" Carl asked back.

"No, I was at Fort Donelson. I've been trying to get home for weeks after it fell. I've been hiding from Union patrols ever since."

"You were in a battle?" Carl asked.

"I think so," Kyle said, once again scanning the area for more troops.

"Did you kill anyone?" Carl asked.

Kyle paused, "Look, it's dark. Come home with me. It's not far. I think we can get there by midnight."

"I've got to get back to my unit!" Carl said.

"I know, me too, but you'll never find them tonight. Worse yet, they might shoot either one of us in the dark. Come home with me. I want you to meet my sister. We can figure out what to do in the morning. We'll both find our way back to our own sides then."

"Man, I don't know…" Carl slumped his shoulders.

"Need I remind you, you are my prisoner," Kyle said in a feigned serious tone.

"Prisoner?!" Carl spurted.

"I did best you in that fight," Kyle offered.

"You cheated, you redneck yokel," Carl said, extending his arm out for help.

Kyle laughed, grabbing Carl's hand pulling him to his feet, "There's my old friend."

They dusted themselves off and adjusted their uniforms. Carl reached over to fix Kyle's collar. That's when he saw the dirt covered gold bar that adorned it.

"Lieutenant?! How did you get to be a Lieutenant?" Carl gasped with a little outrage.

Kyle chuckled, scanning his friend's uniform, "Well, ummm *Private* Smith, maybe you joined the wrong side."

"I didn't want to join any side," Carl mumbled defeatedly.

"I know, what the hell are you doing in the Army?" Kyle asked.

"It's a long story…" Carl said, looking off to the trail from where he had come from.

"We've got all night," Kyle said.

"Oh, no, I really should get back. They'll hang me as a deserter."

"Clearly they won't," Kyle said, "you're my prisoner!"

Carl lifted an eyebrow.

"And I outrank you," Kyle added.

"I'm only going to tolerate so much of that," Carl said.

"Listen, Carl, you're the first friendly face I've seen in months. I've been through a lot. I'm going home to check in on my family before I return to duty. As far as anyone knows, I either died or was captured at Fort Donelson. The same goes for you right now." Kyle put his hands on his buddy's shoulder. "For one night let's forget about this war and remember our friendship. I told you I've always wanted to show you my home. We may never get this chance again. Come with me. I'll get you back to your Union Army. It'll be fine. Besides, there's no way you're making your way back there tonight."

Carl let out a long sigh, "Alright, then."

"That's my boy!" Kyle punched him in the arm, "Come on, you're just going to adore my sister! So how did you end up in the Army?"

"Girl trouble," Carl responded.

Chapter Eight: Friends and Enemies

The two rode for hours through the woods. They tried to be as quiet as possible, fearing patrols from either side. But the two friends could not contain themselves for long. They had so much to talk about since they last parted. So they spoke in hushed tones as they made their way, quieting themselves at any odd sound they heard. But the need to learn each other's story up to that point kept the conversation going.

Carl told Kyle about bumping into their old archenemy from school, Klaus Schmidt, at the train station and the duel that followed.

"Good God! You chopped his hand off?!" Kyle blurted.

"No, I merely pierced it. It was an accident. They had to remove it later," Carl answered. He told Kyle how the duel had led to his arrest and subsequent impressment into the Army.

"Well, at least we don't have to deal with that asshole anymore," Kyle offered.

"No kidding, what a jerk!" Carl replied. The two had a giggle at the unyielding German immigrant's expense.

Kyle told his story about how he went into service immediately upon returning home. That his father arranged his commission and, for the most part, he had been a courier running messages from one officer to another. He told him how he had been sent from New Madrid to Bowling Green and then to Fort Donelson. Carl was amazed at the story of the battle and breakout. Kyle neglected to tell him about his fight with the Union horseman and how he got the horse he was currently riding. He felt ashamed that he was holding back from his friend, but he just couldn't find the nerve to talk about it.

The trek was a hard go. They spent hours making their way through the dark woods. Doubt and fear haunted Carl as they went on. *Have I made a big mistake?* kept creeping into his mind. *Does he even know where we're going?* He was about to suggest they stop for the night when they came to the river.

"Ah, yes!" Kyle piped up, "Here it is! We're not far now. There's a ferry that'll take us to the Tennessee side, and then we're only about an hour from home."

They went down to the landing where a small shack stood near a flat-bottomed raft that was tied to a launch. They knocked lightly, as there was no light coming from inside. They were about to give up when an old man came to the door in his long johns holding a shotgun. The man looked at the two boys in their opposing uniforms and said, "Isn't a little late for you boys to be out on a date?"

"We have money; we need to get across sir," Kyle said. The man looked at them for a moment and then shrugged.

"Gimme a minute," he said, disappearing into the dark shed. The boys led their horses onto the raft and waited. The man appeared moments later. He still had his shotgun, but merely carried it to the raft and set it down as he untied the moorings. "You can never be too sure these days," the man said. The boys murmured in obligatory agreement. "Aren't you Bethune's boy?"

"Yes, I am," Kyle answered, "I'm surprised you remember me, Mr. Roberts."

"You were just a pup last time I saw you," the old man said, "still are! That uniform doesn't fool me." The old man produced a bottle of amber liquid from his coat jacket and handed it to Kyle. "How's your dad?" he asked, as he started poling the raft across the river.

Kyle took a pull from the bottle, shuddered, and then let out a satisfied "ahhhh." "He's fine, sir. Last I knew he went to New Orleans to try to get our cotton past the blockade." He handed the bottle to Carl, "The English are willing to pay for it more than ever!"

"What about you, Billy Yank," the old man eyed Carl harshly, "why are you in my country?"

"I'm wondering the same thing," Carl said. He took a swig from the bottle. The liquid was like silk and fire at the same time. It had an earthy, nutty taste with a hint of vanilla, "My God, but that's good!"

"Tennessee whiskey, boy," Mr. Roberts grunted, "the best in the world. Now I asked you a question, why are you invading my land?"

Carl looked at him with his mouth agape, lost for words. Kyle intervened, "Carl is a friend of mine. We go to school together. He's my guest."

"You a Mexican or a Yankee?" the old man asked.

"What?!" Carl asked.

"Mr. Roberts fought in the Mexican War, Carl. Sometimes he can't tell his enemies apart in the dark," Kyle offered with humor, trying to defuse the moment as he took the bottle from Carl's hand and handed it back to the old man.

"My mother's French, sir," Carl said, "her family's from the south of France, a more Mediterranean clime. She says some of the people there are a bit on the tan side, sir."

The old man took a pull from the whiskey. It seemed to have no effect on the scrutinizing stare he gave Carl.

"My dad fought in the Mexican War too, sir," Carl bumbled, trying to find common ground.

"On whose side?"

Both boys' eyebrows arched in surprise.

"Well, on ours, of course!" Carl stammered, "...or what used to be both of ours at that time, I guess..."

"I see," the old man handed Carl the bottle back, "what's his name?"

"His name was David Smith. I believe he was a lieutenant. He didn't survive the war," Carl said, taking a pull from the bottle.

"Well, you go prancing around these parts in that uniform, you ain't going to survive this one neither."

Mr. Roberts hesitated before taking the money from Kyle once they reached the other side. He shrugged and then pocketed the coins. "Times are tough, son," he said. "You're daddy's a good man, please give him my regards."

"I will, Mr. Roberts," Kyle said putting his hand on the old man's shoulder.

"And say hi to that pretty sister of yours," Mr. Roberts added and then thought for a minute, "and that pretty little negro she always has with her."

"Liza, yes, she'll be glad to hear from you," Kyle responded.

The old man regarded Kyle for a moment. His eyes seemed to glisten over with moisture. Then he patted Kyle on the shoulder and said, "May God have mercy on us all," before returning to the raft and pushing off into the dark water alone.

Kyle's estimate proved to be right. It took the boys about an hour from there to reach the Bethune Plantation. There was no mistaking that they had arrived when Kyle led Carl under the arch that held his family's name. The arch spanned across two stone columns that also supported an iron gate. On the other side of the gate was a well-groomed gravel lane that, in the darkness, appeared to shoot through a tunnel which Carl assumed to be a canopy of trees. As they made their way through the dark "tunnel," Kyle's home began to come into full view. What first looked like a white blur revealed itself to be a grand house. It had two full floors with a large veranda on the first floor and balconies on the second. Even the sloped roof atop had gabled windows suggesting a partial third floor. Attached to the side of the giant home seemed to be another full-sized house. "That's the kitchen," Kyle said, pointing to it, "I'm sure we'll find something to eat before we bed down for the night."

Carl was stunned by the opulence of Kyle's home. Even in the darkness, it seemed to overflow with wealth. They went through a corridor that led to the kitchen. It was a large room surrounded by glass windows that could fill it full of sunlight during the day. Kyle struck a match and lit a lantern. "Take a seat here," he motioned to a large wooden table in the center of the room. "Let me see what we've got here…" he said, checking the cupboards, "ah! They seem to have been made today!"

Kyle came back with a hand full of biscuits, some ham, and a jar of honey. "Help yourself, my friend. I'm going into the cellar to get us a decent bottle."

"Wow, thanks!" Carl said, his eyes trying to take in everything the lamplight revealed. The biscuits were softer than anything he had eaten in months. He started carving on the ham when he was interrupted by the click of a gun.

"You Yankees sure like to make yourselves at home, raiding our properties like this," a woman's voice said.

Carl looked up to see the two barrels of a shotgun pointed at him. Behind the barrels was a toss of wild red hair and green eyes framed by a beautifully sculpted freckled face.

"Ma'am!" Carl tried to speak with a mouth full of biscuit, "I'm a friend of your brother!"

"All I see is a Yankee invader helping himself to my family's food," Kathryn said, holding the gun steady on Carl.

"Kathryn!" Kyle reappeared from the cellar with a bottle of wine in his hand. "It's alright, he's with me!"

Kathryn looked at him and then back at Carl before lowering the gun. "You are out of your mind bringing this man into our home at this time of night! A Yankee?! Have you lost your senses? I could have shot you both. I still ought to," she said, raising the gun again at Carl. Carl threw his hands up, his eyes wide with alarm.

"Kathryn, Kathryn…please, let me explain," Kyle pleaded.

"You better! If Mamma found out you brought a Yankee into our home she'd have your hide!"

"Come, let's not fuss in front of our guest," Kyle tried to lead her out of the room.

"Our guest?! These monsters have been raiding our homes, defiling our women, shooting our boys! He's our guest?!" Kathryn shot back. "We better shoot him now. Aren't we in a war?"

"Come, now," Kyle said calmly, "let's talk." He put his hand on her shoulder, causing her to lower the gun. Carl wasn't sure if he was more stunned by her beauty or her ferociousness. She gave him a glance as they left the room.

"Don't you try to steal anything, Billy Yank. I'm watching you!" She said as they walked out the door.

Carl sat there in stunned silence as he listened to the siblings move down the corridor to the main house, their conversation now becoming muffled and unrecognizable. He sat there for a minute and then, with a shrug, decided to return to cutting the ham. The meat was so tender and juicy Carl had to stop himself from drooling. It had been so long since he had anything so good. He realized he hadn't eaten since before he went out for vedette duty earlier in the day. He put the slice of ham on a biscuit and was drawing it to his mouth when he noticed a pair of eyes watching him from the darkness in the hallway.

"Sweet Jesus!" Carl jumped. The eyes walked into the glow of the lantern to reveal a young black woman dressed in a simple white gown.

"Oh, I'm sorry. Did I scare you, Mr. Yankee Soldier, sir?" the woman said with no lack of irony.

"I'm sorry...I'm just a little...I wasn't expecting you," Carl said looking at the young woman in awe. *My God, she's beautiful too!* he thought.

"Well, I certainly didn't expect to see you either, sir," she said crossing her arms in contempt. "What do you Yankees think you're doing down here anyway? Causing all this trouble."

"We're here to save you," Carl offered.

"Oh, you're going to save me?" she said.

"Well, yeah...I mean your people," Carl stammered.

"My people?" Liza put her hand on her chest.

"Yeah...you know...from slavery and stuff," Carl tried.

"Okay, then what?" she said crossing her arms.

"*Then* what? What do you mean?" Carl asked.

"Okay, everything is fine..." Kyle said, stepping back into the room. He then stopped in his tracks and gazed at Liza. She unfolded her arms and looked back into his soft, blue eyes, her own eyes softening. Carl sat there confused in the silence that ensued, watching the two regard each other.

"Wait a minute..." Carl mumbled.

"I'm sorry," Kyle snapped from his reverie, "Carl, this is Miss Liza; Liza, this is Mr. Smith."

"Call me Carl, please," Carl said, rising from his chair. Liza raised an eyebrow.

"They're a lot less formal in the North, Liza," Kyle tried to explain.

"I see," Liza said turning away, "I'll prepare a room for him."

"Thank you, Liza," Kyle smiled, trying to restore a sense of civility to the room.

"...And a washbowl," she added, as she walked away, "he stinks."

"Liza!" Kyle groaned, but she was already gone. "I'm really sorry," Kyle turned to Carl, "they're just frightened because of the war and all..." Carl just stared back at him, a slight smile growing across his face. "What...?" Kyle asked.

"You're sweet on her," Carl stated, his smile now full. Kyle let out a sigh. "You rascal!" Carl chuckled.

"Please, not a word to anyone," Kyle pleaded.

"Of course!" Carl brightened with delight.

"We all grew up together. Liza and her brother were almost like siblings to us. She and my sister are inseparable," Kyle explained.

"But she's a little more than a sister to you, isn't she?" Carl asked, enjoying his friend's discomfort.

"I'm afraid so," Kyle said, looking down at his hands. Then he brought his big, blue eyes to meet Carl's. "I love her, Carl," he said, and then dropped his eyes back to his hands, "I love her dearly..."

Carl paused for a moment, watching his friend in anguish. "I understand," he said at last, "it's certainly going to make for an interesting war..."

Kyle laughed, " I suppose you're right. I'll have to sort it all out at some point."

They talked, ate, and finished off the bottle of red wine that Kyle had brought from the cellar. Kyle then led him to his room. A porcelain washbowl had been set on the dresser along with a bar of soap, a rag, a towel, and a sleep shirt. The water was still warm. It was a welcomed luxury in the cold night's air. Having cleaned himself enough to his satisfaction, Carl slipped into the nightshirt and crawled into the large feather bed that was framed by large oak posts. He pulled the down-stuffed comforter over his shoulders and closed his eyes. He had never felt anything so comfortable in his life.

His eyes popped open with the squeak of the door. He reached for his pistol and then realized he had stupidly left on the dresser. He snapped his eyes back to the door. Lit by a single candle stood Kathryn. Carl was stunned to see her standing there in her white cotton shirt drawn in by a bodice that revealed her slender waist. Ruffles spilled out of the bodice and extended over her white cotton drawers that ended at her knees where white stockings took over to cover her legs down to her feet.

She walked over to the bed setting her candle down on the nightstand. She sat on the bed and started removing her stockings.

"What are you doing?" Carl gasped.

"Don't get any funny ideas, Billy Yank," she said, "these are hard times and it's cold." She removed her bodice, blew out the candle, and then crawled into bed. She lay on her side with her back to him. She turned for a moment, looked at him, then grabbed his arm and wrapped it around her.

Carl lay there stunned for a moment. Then felt the embarrassment of his arousal growing in the space between them. He tried to fight it, but holding her soft delicate body next to his was excruciating, so he hoped she wouldn't notice.

"Good Lord! Neither of us is going to get any sleep with that thing!" she exclaimed.

"I'm sorry…it's been so long…" Carl stammered in his shame.

"Why don't you go to the watershed and take care of your business then?" she demanded.

"What…?"

"Oh, for crying out loud," she hissed, "you men are all the same, can't do anything yourselves!" She turned over and Carl felt her cold hand sheath over his manhood.

"Oh, my goodness," he stammered, "I'm sorry… it's been so long…I might make a mess."

"Don't worry, sweetheart, I have a hankie," she said softly. That's all it took. He exploded with withering ecstasy. "Wow! That didn't take long," she giggled. "What a mess!"

"I'm sorry…I…" Carl tried to say something that made sense.

"Hush, darling." She got up and cleaned her hand and arm off in the wash basin, then tossed the hankie to the floor. She crawled back in bed, pulling his arm over again and said, "Now go to sleep."

Carl closed his eyes and felt himself falling into a black pit. The exhaustion, the food, the wine, the sexual release, the plush bed, and the small warm body pressed to his was more than a match for his consciousness. He was out immediately.

It took several hours to wake in the morning. The first time only a hint of light was creeping through the window, as the sun had not yet risen. Kathryn still lay there, soundly asleep. *So it wasn't a dream,* Carl thought. He closed his eyes again. The next time he opened them she was gone. More light was coming into the room now. It was gray and dreary. A soft patter of rain began. Carl groaned, rolled away from the window, and went back to sleep.

The room was full of gray light and rain smacked against the window when Carl woke again. He sat on the side of the bed for a moment blinking his eyes and rubbing the back of his neck. He then stood. A fresh wash bowl had been set out for him. He splashed his face and rinsed his mouth out. His uniform was gone. "Hmmmmm…" he pondered. On the dresser was a neatly stacked set of civilian clothes: socks, drawers, suspenders, a clean shirt, brown wool trousers, and a matching vest. He listened carefully as he dressed. The murmuring of a conversation below was the sign of life he was listening for.

"Well, they grow them awfully lazy up in the North, don't they?" Liza quipped as Carl entered the parlor, still buttoning his vest.

"What time is?" Carl said, rubbing the back of his neck.

"It's a little past ten," Kathryn smirked at him, "you must have been plenty tired from all that activity last night."

"Good Lord, I'm in trouble!" Carl exclaimed.

"Easy, Carl," Kyle said, "we'll get you back safely to your Army. You can say you were captured, but escaped."

"God, I hope they buy it!" He flopped in a chair. Liza poured him a cup of coffee and handed it to him.

"I think there's some bacon and eggs left in the kitchen; I'll bring you some," she said.

"Thank you," Carl said, watching her leave the room, and then to Kyle and his sister, "How are we going to get me back?"

"We'll work it out, but…um," Kyle stammered uncomfortably.

"What my brother is trying to say," Kathryn jumped in, "is that we need your help."

Carl gazed openmouthed at the two siblings, "Oh, boy, I'm in trouble…"

Chapter Nine: The Plan

"You are out of your minds..." Carl said, looking at the three Southerners.

"It's really quite simple. It should only take a day or two. Then you can go back to your regiment and continue killing us," Kathryn said mildly.

"You want me to help you get back one of your runaway slaves? Isn't that exactly what I'm fighting against?" Carl asked incredulously.

"He's not just some slave," Liza interjected, putting her hand on Kyle's shoulder as she stood behind him in his chair.

Kyle looked up at her and cupped her hand with his own. Then he returned his gaze to Carl, "She's right, he's family."

"Then why did he run away?" Carl asked blankly.

Kyle sighed, "Because he wanted to be free. Just like anyone else, I suppose." An uneasy silence took hold of the room. No one wanted to look at anyone else in the eye. Kathryn was the first to speak.

"Look, he is a lot worse off now than he ever was here. True, Elijah was our slave, but we loved him, we cared about him. I'm told now he is suffering terrible hardships under the whip of those fools trying to turn New Madrid into a fortress," she said.

"Why don't you just go there and claim him if he belongs to you?" Carl asked.

"We wish it were that easy." Kyle shook his head looking down at his hands.

"We tried," Kathryn said. "I've written letters to the mayor, the governor, and some of the military leaders there. The ones that have responded say the Confederacy needs every resource that's available if we are going to defend ourselves from the Yankee invasion. They say everyone must make sacrifices. Our father is a powerful man. I've asked him to intervene, but he says the same thing. He's too busy trying to sell our cotton in New Orleans before the Yankees seize it."

"Won't they just return him when the war is over?" Carl asked.

"He'll die, sir," Liza let out a sob, sniffed, and then gathered herself. She then spoke steadily, trying to hold the emotions that threatened to render her into uncontrollable tears. "We slaves communicate, you see. We got people all over, everywhere. They talk. They pass messages. We got families split up, sent to different states even, but we keep up. We communicate the best we can, sir."

She took a moment to frame what she was going to say next. "My connections tell me they've seen my brother. He's at New Madrid, helping build their defenses. They are working them to death under the lash. They are running out of food. Even the white soldiers are going without. They don't care about the slaves. They're working them and working them. Men are dying every day by the dozens, many going down with the fever, many just too weak to live. Still, they're working them. If Elijah stays there, it'll be his end. He's a sweet boy, sir. He's got the most beautiful heart

God's ever given a man." She let out a sob, "He's my baby brother…"

And then the tears came. She didn't look away. She held her eyes on Carl's. The weight of her sorrow was crushing him. Below her sat Kyle. His face was buried in his hands. He was crying too. Carl looked to Kathryn. Silent tears rolled down her face. She looked away as if something outside of the window caught her attention.

Carl let out a sigh. "And why do you need me?" he asked softly.

"Because no one knows you," Kathryn answered. "They would recognize my brother immediately."

"Yeah, they're probably wondering where I've been. I'd have to make an accounting for myself of what I've been doing since Captain Gray sent me off to Kentucky to plea for more troops. All eyes would be on me."

"But no one knows you," Kathryn continued, "you could escort Liza and me to town. It would be unbecoming for a young lady to travel alone with just her maid. Liza and I could get close to Elijah. Once we've found him, we'll figure a way to get him from the others and smuggle him out of town. We will need your help…and your protection, of course."

"I'll be waiting just outside of town with horses," Kyle said. "We'll take him back home and you then can rejoin your regiment. Sikeston is just up the road from there. You can say you were captured, which…is more or less true."

"That is if our troops haven't already started the assault on New Madrid…" Carl said.

"All the more reason to get him out now, sir," Liza said. "Those bombs don't know who is who when they fall."

Carl looked up at Kathryn who smirked and gave him a wink. He sighed, "Okay, I'll do it."

"Oh, sir! I cannot thank you enough!" Liza ran over to Carl, taking his hand with both of hers. She knelt at his chair. Kyle got up and walked over to him, placing a hand on his shoulder.

"I will owe you an enormous debt..." he started.

"Oh, stop," Carl cut him off, "you knew I was going to say yes."

"How are we going to hide that dreadful accent?" Kathryn chimed in.

"How about this," Carl said, and then in his best attempt at a Southern drawl, "Howdy, y'all!"

"Oh, dear heavens!" Kathryn gasped.

"You probably better off not talking at all," Liza said, getting up, her composure now returning.

Much had to be thought out that day. First, no one was to know the two boys were at the Bethune Plantation. Kyle could be shot as an absconder, and Carl could be hanged as a spy. Kathryn would send a message to Mr. Johnson, the overseer, that she and Liza would be going to town to visit friends for a few days and do a little shopping. What she wouldn't tell him is that they weren't going to nearby Tiptonville on the Tennessee side, but to New Madrid much farther away. A place that at the moment was a hornets' nest of military activity. A place the Federals were approaching fast, a very dangerous place indeed.

Kathryn would refuse a driver, claiming that she and Liza could handle the small wagon themselves. Kyle and Carl would leave separately under the cover of darkness in the early morning. They would stay off the roads and hide in the woods just south of town until the girls met up with them. Then Carl would ride into town with them as their escort. Kathryn would claim he was a visiting cousin from out of state. They'd find Elijah and smuggle him back to the meeting place. Carl would then leave to rejoin his ranks. Kyle would see his sister, Liza, and Elijah home safe before returning to duty himself.

The four spent a happy afternoon together in the house. The rain kept any visitors away, so with their parents gone and most of their servants with them, the four friends had the rule of the house. Carl and Kyle didn't need to hide. Kyle and Liza were openly affectionate with each other. Carl and Kathryn flirted. The diminished kitchen staff came, did their work, and left, never venturing into the main house. Yet each of them knew that this happy moment was fleeting, that in mere hours the fantasy would be over. The heartache and suffering would return. Still, they all tried to hide this feeling of dread from each other as the sun set and the evening meal was enjoyed. Then it was time for bed.

"We'll have to get up quite early tomorrow," Kyle said, finishing off his glass of wine.

"I suppose so," Carl agreed, finishing his glass as well.

Kyle gave Liza a sly smile and then turned back to Carl, "I'll come get you a few hours before sunrise."

"Alright," Carl said, then looked to Kathryn. She didn't return his gaze.

"I'll have the kitchen crew come clean this up in the morning," Kathryn said, getting up, "goodnight, gentlemen, goodnight, Liza." With that, she stood up, put her napkin down, and walked out of the room.

"Goodnight, Miss Kathryn," Liza said watching her leave while giving Kyle a peck on the cheek.

"Good night," the two boys murmured.

"I suppose I'll be going off too," Kyle said, a little embarrassed over how obvious it was that Liza would be joining him.

Carl let out a light laugh and shook his head, "Yeah, me too, I suppose."

The two lovers scampered off, giggling and speaking in low voices to each other. Carl felt a pang of loneliness. He was tempted to pour himself another glass of wine but thought better of it. Tomorrow morning would come soon. He took a candle and made his way to his room.

His uniform had been washed and neatly bundled with twine next to a fresh washing bowl that had been set out for him. Sitting on top of his clothes was the gold chain and locket Anna had given him. "Hmmmmm…" he said to himself. *They must have found it in my pocket when they washed my clothes.* Carl opened it and looked at the plump-faced beauty with golden curls and large, innocent, blue eyes. Carl snapped the locket shut.

"Who is she?" a voice came in the darkness.

"Jesus Christ!" Carl jumped.

"A sweetheart from back home?" Kathryn sat up in the bed.

"My God, but I felt my spirit leave my body just now…" Carl said, putting his hand to his beating heart.

"Well?" Kathryn cocked an eyebrow.

"No…well, sort of…but not really…oh, I don't know…" Carl slumped down on the bed letting his shoulders drop.

"Let me help you," Kathryn started unbuttoning his vest. "Do you want to tell me about it?"

Carl did his best to explain how he came into possession of the photograph of the lovesick little sister of his archenemy as Kathryn undressed him and led him back to the wash bowl where she bathed him with the wash rag. The sensation was unreal. He tried to explain how Anna was the cause of all his problems as he tried to contain the maddening desire he was feeling for Kathryn. He did his best to hide that deep down, he thought Anna was cute, and that he may have been developing feelings for her after all he'd been through. But tonight he could not believe he was here with, what may have been, the most beautiful woman he had ever seen.

"Sounds like a nice girl," Kathryn said, her green eyes shining in the candlelight.

"Yeah, she's alright," Carl said, as he leaned in and kissed her for the very first time. Kathryn wrapped her arms around him, kissing him fully. She moved her lips down his neck and then to his bare shoulder.

"You have a dark complexion, unlike the men down here. Is that typical of the Northern men? Are you all mixed?" she asked.

Carl laughed, "No, I get that a lot, though. I'm half French. My mother's family comes from the Mediterranean side. That's where I get it from."

"Is she as dark as you?"

"No, but I don't think it works that way. Shoot…I don't know,"

They blew out the candle and lay down together entwined in each other's arms. "I won't let you deflower me, Billy Yank." She could sense his defeat, "But we can do things to make each other happy, nonetheless." Carl smiled and kissed her neck, "You could end up dying in my service tomorrow for all we know."

"Then I would die a happy man," Carl said.

The knock came lightly at the door. Carl moved his hand around the bed looking for Kathryn. She was gone. The door creaked open and Kyle's head appeared, "Hey, are you ready?"

Carl sat up rubbing his eyes, "I guess."

"I've got some hot coffee for you," Kyle came in offering him a cup of steamy liquid.

"You are a true friend," Carl said, as he took the cup and sipped.

"No, Carl, you are," Kyle said earnestly.

"Okay, don't get mushy on me."

Their horses had already been packed and ready to go when they got to the stables. The day of rest and eating had done much for the two animals after the hard journey they had two nights before. Carl tucked his uniform into one of his saddlebags. He checked his saber and revolving carbine before securing them in their saddle holsters. He holstered his pistol on his hip and then covered it with the civilian jacket that matched his suit.

Kyle was also out of uniform. He wore civilian clothes as well. He kept his beard to hide his face and hoped they would not encounter anyone who knew him.

They rode in the dark. The road was mostly mud, so riding in the cover of the woods actually made the trip a bit easier. They made it to an obscure ferry crossing by daybreak. Kyle said this one would be much safer than the busier crossings at Point Pleasant or New Madrid because of all the frantic military activity going on. The ferryman eyed the boys suspiciously but accepted Kyle's money nonetheless. Carl made sure to keep his mouth shut and not betray his Yankee accent. Once across the river, they rode north towards New Madrid until they came to their designated meeting place, just a few miles south of town and out of sight of the Rebel pickets that were set out to watch the roads for a Union advance. They found a dry spot in the woods just off the road and waited…and waited.

It seemed like they waited all day. They could see supplies and couriers running from New Madrid down to the defenses the Rebels were building at Point Pleasant. By the afternoon they were beginning to worry. They debated whether one of them should ride towards Point Pleasant to try to find the girls and who that one should be. Finally, Kyle spotted the small horse-drawn wagon with the two girls riding on the bench. The boys came out to greet them and then pulled the wagon off the road into the woods, out of view of the passersby.

"What took you so long?" Kyle asked.

"Oh, we had a dreadful time getting away," Kathryn said, "Mr. Johnson was most insistent that we stay home or that he go with us. I know he was just worried for our safety. In the end, I had to get short with him, but it's all for the better good, I suppose. In the meantime, I put the kitchen to work." With that, she pulled back a gingham cloth that covered one of the many baskets that were stacked in the back of the wagon. The smell immediately rushed over the boys causing them to salivate. Carl made to pick up one of the sweet cornbread cakes that were stuffed in the basket. Kathryn slapped his hand away. "Ah, ah, ah…," she snapped, "those are for *our* boys." Carl and Kyle looked at her with boyish disappointment. Kathryn let out a sigh, "Men are such children! Okay, you can each have one, but these are our passage into town."

The boys greedily snatched up their cakes before Liza returned the cloth. "We have something else," Liza said. She handed Carl a cane.

"What's this?" Carl said.

"You'll see," Liza said, as she produced a roll of gauze from the cart. She rolled up one of Carl's pant legs and started bandaging his leg. She finished by wrapping some of the gauze around his neck. "Now all we have to do is get you to keep your mouth shut," she said, satisfied with her work.

Carl climbed into the wagon. Kyle helped him in. "I'll be waiting here. There's a landing straight back through the woods. If you can't get him out on the wagon, you might be able to steal a skiff under the cover of night. The current will bring you right there."

Liza blew him a kiss as she slapped the reigns. The three were back on the road, on their way to New Madrid. Carl couldn't help but to consider the madness they were about to try. *We have not properly thought this through,* he thought, as they approached the Confederate vedette set on the road. Carl felt his stomach tighten with fear as a gray-clad officer nudged his horse to the wagon. The officer looked hard at Liza and Carl with his piercing green eyes before his gaze fell on Kathryn. His clean-shaven face broke into a smile. "What brings you so far from home, Miss Bethune?" he asked slyly.

"Lathan," Kathryn returned the smile, "it's good to see they've put your, ummm…*talents* to good use."

"Everybody's got to be good at something, I suppose," he said just as sweetly, then dropped his smile, "why are you here?"

"Well, there's only one thing I'm good at," Kathryn said, pouring more sweetness into her voice. She pulled back the cloth that covered some of the corn cakes, "…and that's Southern hospitality." Lathan regarded the cakes for a moment. "Go ahead," she smiled, "take one!"

"No, thanks," Lathan returned his eyes to her and smiled again.

"Well, perhaps your men would like some. We made them for the troops," Kathryn said. Some of Lathan's men moved towards the wagon. One of them leaned from his saddle stretching his hand towards the cakes. Lathan pushed his hand away without looking.

"They're fine. These men are on duty. They're not having a tea party," Lathan said. He turned his eyes to Carl. "Who's this?"

"That's my cousin, Carl, from Texas," Kathryn answered, "he's convalescing with us after being wounded at Fort Donelson."

Lathan scanned Carl again, "How were you wounded, soldier?"

Carl gulped, "I…ah…"

Kathryn put her hand on his mouth, "He really shouldn't talk. The poor thing had bomb fragments pulled out of his leg and throat."

"I see…" Lathan said. "How come he isn't in Nashville with the rest of the men who ran away from the fight?" Carl started moving his hand towards his pistol under his jacket. Liza put her hand on his to stop him.

"Because he has family here," Kathryn said, dropping her sweetness as she was beginning to get annoyed with the endless questions. Carl looked from her to him and then to the other Confederate soldiers. He wondered how many of them he could shoot before they pulled out their own guns.

Lathan paused for a moment and then said, "Perhaps when this war is over I could call upon you, Miss Bethune."

Kathryn turned the charm back on, fluttering her eyes, "Why that would be marvelous, Mr. Woods! Please do!"

Lathan smiled, "Oh, I intend to, ma'am, I intend to." With that, he made a grand gesture with his hand to let them pass. Liza wasted no time prodding the horse on. Lathan sat on his horse smiling, watching them as they rode towards Fort Thompson, the city's southern-most defense.

Getting into Fort Thompson was far easier than getting past Lathan Woods and his men. The hungry sentries were more than happy to let the three in with their delicious treats. The only thing stopping the men from devouring all of them was that Kathryn claimed they were for General McCown, the new commanding officer at New Madrid, but the boys at Fort Thompson could have a few.

The attention the beautiful redhead with her sweet cornbread cakes was enough of a distraction for Liza to walk among the slaves and ask questions. Carl was immensely uncomfortable being surrounded by so many enemy soldiers. He felt he would lose his composure at any minute and start running. The story of his injured throat was a blessing of an excuse to keep him from having to answer questions and possibly blow their cover.

Kathryn was beginning to run out of reasons why the men at Fort Thompson couldn't devour all the cakes when Liza came back and quietly took her place at the reigns. "Okay, I know where he is," she whispered.

"Okay, boys!" Kathryn told them, "We must be on our way." Liza gave the reigns a slap and with that, they were headed into town.

Chapter Ten: The Rescue

New Madrid was a swarm of activity. Men, horses, and carriages ran up and down mud-filled Main Street all the way to the river. There, Confederate mortar rafts and gunboats patrolled the waters waiting for the Federal ironclads to come steaming down the river at any given minute. In every direction, slaves worked on the earthen ramparts put in place to protect the city from an imminent land assault.

Just east of the landing, another fort stood. Slaves scurried around it like ants as their overseers prodded them with the threat of whips and clubs.

"That's got to be it," Liza murmured to the others.

"I'll set up here. Trust me, every man here is going to be more interested in what I've got in these baskets than you two poking around," Kathryn smiled.

"I'll be back," Liza said and off she went towards the fort.

"I'll walk her to the fort and then check around the river for a boat we can steal," Carl said, as he climbed out of the wagon with his cane.

"Don't forget to keep your mouth shut," Kathryn said. "One word with that filthy Northern accent and the jig is up."

"Don't worry," Carl smiled, "I've got this under control," he said with a wink.

"Hmph," Kathryn said, "famous last words…" She waited for the two to make their way across the street before calling attention to herself. "Oh, my stars, does anyone here know where I'm supposed to deliver these cornbread cakes?" It didn't take long for her to be surrounded by men competing to be the most helpful. The redhead beauty commanded so much attention, that few bothered to pay any attention to the pretty young black woman or the injured man with a cane that escorted her.

Fifteen feet from the fort Liza turned to Carl, "Good luck, Carl." Carl smiled at the sudden informality.

"Thank you, but I think you have the harder task," Carl returned the smile.

"Me? I'm a slave. I spent my whole life sneakin' around doing things I ought not to."

Carl squeezed her hand, "See you soon!" he whispered and the two parted. Carl made his way to the riverside and watched Liza go to the entrance. She was stopped by the sentries there. Carl held his breath as she pulled back the cover of her basket. The two men helped themselves to some of the cakes and in she went.

Liza scanned the inside of the fort as quickly as she could, looking for her brother. Everywhere, shoeless and shirtless men labored on the high dirt walls or rolled heavy cannons into place under the direction of their white overseers. The occasional crack of a whip made her jump as some bossman chided his team for going too slow.

Liza was guided to the commander's office where she explained that her mistress had sent the treats she had in the basket. The commander was delighted.

"You say the Bethune Plantation?" he asked.

"Yes, sir. Miss Kathryn wanted to do her best to help the war effort, sir," Liza said.

"Ah, well, it's much appreciated. Welcome to Fort Bankhead…ummm…what is your name, Miss?" the commander asked.

"Miss Liza, sir," she said with the same practiced sweetness she and Kathryn used to get their way at the plantation.

"Well, aren't you a pretty, young thing, Miss Liza. I am Colonel Lucius Marshall Walker, at your service, Miss," the officer twinkled at her.

"Would you like to see the fort?"

"Oh, would I!" she exclaimed in the most honeyed voice she could muster.

"Come, let me show you."

Once again, Liza scanned the grounds, trying to find her brother among the toiling slaves.

"Heave you big, dumb, plow horse!" an overseer heckled, drawing Liza and her escort's attention. A team of horses was pulling a heavy cannon into position using a system of ropes and pulleys. At the head of the team was a large man who had put his head through one of the harnesses, and with his shoulder, added his enormous strength to the struggling horses. His bare feet slid in the mud along with the horses' slipping hooves. This was a great source of entertainment for the overseers, who idly watched the work. Liza let out a gasp as she recognized the large man in the horse collar as her little brother.

Colonel Walker sensed her distress at Elijah's treatment. "Oh, him," he tried to soothe her, "he is a wizard with horses, but the boy insists on working alongside them. I suppose he won't ask them to do anything he's not willing to do himself. Hmmmmm… rather noble of him, I do say." Liza watched her brother in silence. With a last hard shove, he and his team of horses forced the cannon onto its perch overlooking the river. Overseers let out a cheer of triumph. Elijah slipped out the harness and proceeded to pat each horse on the back, whispering sweet things in their ears.

"Good job, boys!" Walker called out. Elijah looked back to acknowledge the praise. His smile turned to shock as he saw his sister, standing next to the bossman. Liza raised her finger to her lips and silently mouthed a "Shhhhh."

Colonel Walker escorted Liza to the gate. He told her that she and her mistress were welcome to visit the fort anytime they wished, "So long as we're not in the middle of a battle, of course!" he added lightly with a chuckle.

Carl watched her leave the fort. He hobbled as quickly as he could to catch up to her, maintaining the illusion of an injury. "Did you see him?"

"Yes, they're using him as a plow horse," she said through clenched teeth without breaking her stride or her forward glare.

"I'm sorry," Carl said, trying to keep up with her as he faked his hobble.

Kathryn's wagon was empty. They stood before it, full of dread. "They've arrested her…" Carl mumbled.

"They wouldn't dare," Liza replied under her breath.

"Oh, there they are!" Kathryn's voice broke their silent panic. The beautiful redhead was escorted by a dashing young lieutenant in gray who held her arm in his as they walked. "Lieutenant Davis here was just now giving me a tour of the town's defenses. I'm certain those rascally Yankees will have more than their match here!"

The lieutenant beamed at the attention Kathryn poured on him. "You must be her cousin, Carl, injured in battle at Fort Donelson, right?" Davis held out his hand to Carl, "Please, do tell me about it, sir!"

Carl was about to speak when Kathryn laid her hand on his chest, "I'm afraid the doctor has discouraged Carl from speaking until his throat heals properly."

"Of course!" Davis replied, "My apologies, sir!"

Carl waved it off to imply no that there was no harm done.

"Lieutenant Davis has gallantly offered his room at the inn tonight for our purposes!" Kathryn said with a flourish of charm.

"Absolutely! You'd have no luck getting a room anywhere near here tonight, anyhow. They're all taken," Davis said. "Besides, it's good for a leader, such as myself, to sleep amongst his men from time to time."

"You are so brave and kind to do so!" Kathryn purred.

"We all must make sacrifices in these terrible times, madam," Davis said nobly. Carl tried his hardest not to roll his eyes. "I would hope that I may call upon you, Miss Kathryn, when this is all over."

"Oh, my!" Kathryn fluttered her eyes, "I'd be most honored!"

Carl wanted nothing more than to punch this handsome young officer in the face for flirting with the object of his newfound affection, but instead, he offered him the best gracious smile he could muster. "Please allow me to walk you to the inn," Davis said grandly.

"By all means, sir!" Kathryn snuggled into his arm. Carl allowed himself a low growl as he feigned a limp behind the two. Liza walked at his side, eyeing him and his agitation with unmasked pleasure.

"What?!" Carl hissed at her between his teeth.

Davis left them in the room he had rented above the tavern after chatting with Kathryn for what seemed like forever to Carl. Carl watched him walk out the door and down the muddy street. "Well, look at this!" he heard Liza say. He turned to see Liza holding an immaculate gray uniform complete with the gold stitching on the sleeves that denoted an artillery officer.

"Perfect!" Kathryn said. "I knew that fool of a peacock would have an extra."

"Wait a minute…" Carl said, as the two women eyed him and then the uniform.

They spent the evening making their plan. Kathryn had a meal and a bottle of wine for the three of them sent to the room, all, of course, on the young officer's tab. Carl told them that he found plenty of small skiffs, or flat-bottomed boats, lying around the launch unattended. Kathryn had a good sense of the town and its defenses from her tour. Liza knew where they were keeping her brother. The plan was simple. Carl would get Elijah out of Fort Bankhead with the help of the uniform, and hopefully, a believable story. He and Elijah would slip into the water in one of the skiffs under the cover of darkness. Then they'd drift downstream, careful not make a splash with a paddle until they were clear of New Madrid.

The girls would ride back to the rendezvous point. They and Kyle would then take the trail to the river and light a small fire to signal where Carl and Elijah should come to shore. The girls thought it was a splendid plan. Carl wasn't so sure.

"I don't know if I can do this. They're going to see right through me," he said worriedly.

"You'll be fine," Kathryn said. "The early morning guards are the ones too dumb to get out of duty. If you just act confident, they'll believe anything you say."

Carl shook his head, "If you say so."

They decided to get as much sleep as they could before launching their plan in the early morning darkness. Carl was disappointed when the girls cuddled up together in the small bunk leaving him to lie on the floor alone. For all he knew, this was going to be his last night alive. He had hoped he could spend it with Kathryn in his arms. He could already hear the girls sleeping before he got the nerve to make a protest, so instead, he lay there. Fear and doubt poked at him, denying him his sleep.

It seemed like he had just dozed off when Liza lightly nudged him, "Come on," she said, "it's time to go." They helped him into the Confederate uniform. It seemed to fit well.

"My, my, do I have an eye for men's sizes!" Kathryn congratulated herself as she eyed Carl in the lieutenant's uniform.

"I'm going to get myself shot," Carl said. He found it ironic that this may be the closest he'd ever come to wearing the rank he thought he deserved. The three made their way through the inn, cringing at every step as they creaked their way down the dark hall to the stairs, and across the parlor. But in a town that was now used to people coming and going at all times, day or night due to the military activity, no one stirred during their early morning exit. Still, they were relieved to be outside in the cold air.

"Okay," Kathryn said, adjusting Carl's collar one last time, "you know what to do." She turned to walk away. Carl stopped her, grabbing her arm.

"Aren't you going to kiss me?" he asked. Kathryn looked to Liza, who smiled and looked away, then turned to Carl and gave him a light kiss on the lips.

"Good luck!" she said, and then walked off with Liza into the darkness.

Carl stood there on the cold, dark street alone for a moment. *I'm an idiot,* he thought.

A single soldier stood at the entrance to Fort Bankhead. Carl was practicing what he was going to say in his head as he approached. The soldier broke his thoughts when he snapped a salute. Carl returned it after a brief hesitation and walked into the fort unchallenged. *My God, is this working?* he thought.

Following Liza's directions, he found what he thought seemed most likely to be the slave quarters. A single guard shivered in a chair next to the door. He jumped to his feet when Carl approached and snapped a salute.

"I'm here for the slave, Elijah," Carl said, in the best confident Southern drawl he could manage.

"At this hour, sir?" the private asked.

"His horse skills are needed at Fort Thompson early this morning. I'm to escort him there immediately," Carl said trying to act official.

"Why?" the soldier asked, seeming sincerely confused at why an officer would come to escort a slave in the middle of the night.

"Goddamnit!" Carl hissed, "To move a fucking cannon, for Christ's sakes!"

"Sorry…I'm sorry, sir, I'll get him right away!" the soldier ducked into the cabin. Carl waited in the cold trying to regain his nerve. Moments later the soldier emerged. Behind him, a large man stepped out wearing nothing more than tattered pants and a blanket wrapped around his shoulders. Steam rolled out of his mouth as he looked down at Carl. "He's all yours, sir!" the soldier said happily.

Carl looked up at the big brown eyes that held him with a slight sense of curiosity. "Thank you," he mumbled and then motioned with his head for the big man to follow him.

"You're not from around here, are you, sir?" the soldier asked.

"No…, I'm…ah…from Texas." Carl said, not daring to stop or turn around.

"Ah!" the soldier said as Carl and Elijah walked away. The guard at the entrance snapped another sharp salute as they passed through. Carl returned it quickly and kept walking.

They were out. It almost seemed too easy. Carl didn't dare say anything to Elijah as he turned towards the collection of boats beached near the fort on the riverfront. He just hoped Liza's brother would know to follow him as odd as it must have seemed.

"A little late to be taking your pet for a walk."

The man's voice behind him raised the hair on the back of his neck. Carl turned to see the smooth-faced, green-eyed Confederate officer he had encountered the day before.

"Kathryn's cousin Carl, right?" Lathan Woods smiled at him, "Injured at Fort Donelson, it was. Am I right?"

"Ah…yes…that's right," Carl said, his mind racing.

"Back in uniform, I see. Seems like you healed up rather quickly! You can talk now too! That's quite a miracle! Funny…you don't sound like you're from Texas. Although, you could pass for a Mexican. I'd hate to think Miss Kathryn would have relations with someone of tainted blood," Lathan circled the two, thoroughly enjoying Carl's anguish.

"I'm half French…you see…" Carl offered.

"Ah, I see," Lathan soothed, "where are you taking this negro then?"

"Um…Fort Thompson, sir, to help move cannons with…um…horses because…he's…umm, good with them…horses, that is…sir…" Carl offered weakly.

"Fort Thompson is in the other direction," Lathan said, dropping his feigned friendliness. "unless you were planning on going there on one of these boats here."

"Well…, um…yeah, that's a great idea," Carl said.

"Let me see your papers," Lathan said flatly.

"Papers?" Carl asked.

"Your orders," Lathan said losing his patience, "unless that is, you don't have any. In that case, I'll have to ask you to come with me. We can clear this up with the commanding officer."

"No, that won't be necessary. I've got them right here," Carl said patting his pants, then without warning, threw a right hook. Lathan blocked the punch with his left arm and rammed his right fist into Carl's stomach, doubling him over. Lathan drew his fist back and then rammed it up into Carl's left eye flipping him on to his back. Next came a boot heel to Carl's groin, curling him into a fetal position.

Carl let out a groan as he heard the cocking of a pistol. "Now, I'll have that US Army issued pistol you're carrying, Billy Yank," Lathan said flatly.

Carl looked up at the gun pointing at him. He was reeling in pain and defeat as he went to unholster and surrender his firearm. A large black fist crossed his field of vision and smashed into the side of Lathan's neck. Lathan dropped to the ground. Elijah squatted next to Carl, gently putting a hand on his shoulder. His large, brown eyes full of concern, "Are you okay, sir?"

"Yeah, thanks," Carl said, groaning as he got up. "We should kill him now while we have the chance."

"We can't do that, sir," Elijah said, "he can't defend himself."

Carl sighed, "Okay, let's at least tie him up. We need to get out of here quick."

They left him gagged and tied to a tree. Lathan glared at them as they carried a small boat to the water, got in, and cast themselves off into the current. Carl watched the ramparts of the fort, waiting for someone to call out a challenge. None came. Elijah watched Carl with concern. He tore off a corner of his blanket and soaked it in the icy water before handing it to Carl, "Put this on your eye, sir," he said softly, "it'll slow down the swelling." Carl looked at the dripping cloth for a moment and then took it.

"Thanks," he said and then hissed in pain as he pressed it to his eye.

Carl felt himself drifting off to sleep as their boat drifted idly down the river in the gray morning light. Elijah's deep voice pulled him out of it. "Is that Liza?" he asked. Carl sat up and looked. On the shore, three people stood near a small fire waving to them.

"Yes, we made it!" Carl said, picking up the oars.

Liza ran up to the boat and threw her arms around her brother. Tears blurred her eyes, "You big dummy!"

Kyle helped Carl out of the boat. "What happened?"

"We got stopped by some guy," he said. He turned to Kathryn, "He's the one we talked to yesterday on our way in."

"Lathan Woods," Kathryn said flatly.

"We tied him up, but I don't think it'll last," Carl said.

"He's a professional tracker," Kathryn said, "it won't be long before he's on us."

"We better go," Kyle said. "Come on Liza, Elijah; we can catch up at home."

"I'm not going with you, Master," Elijah said, straightening himself.

"Elijah!" Liza hissed.

"I'm sorry, but I'm not going with you," Elijah said. Silence passed over the five of them.

"I understand," Kyle said.

"Kyle, no!" Liza gasped.

"I don't know what's right anymore," Kyle said, "but I can't make him go back against his will."

"He can come with me," Carl spoke up. "There are plenty of free blacks working for the Army. He can do that or decide what he wants to do once we're behind our lines."

"I can't thank you enough, Carl," Kyle said embracing his friend.

"I know, but we can figure out a payment plan," Carl said hugging his friend.

Liza looked to her brother, "Try not to do anything this stupid again, Elijah, I can't always come and save you."

"I know, Liza. I promise," Elijah said, hugging his sister.

Carl pulled Kathryn aside as Kyle spoke with Liza and her brother. "I'll come back for you," he said.

Kathryn let out a laugh, "Oh, bless your heart!" she said.

"I mean it, I love you!" he protested.

Kathryn's eyes softened as she looked at him. "I truly care about you, Carl. That's why I'm going to say to you what I've never told any man."

"Okay," Carl gulped.

She put her hand on his face looking with pity at his swollen black eye, "You are certainly pretty, but I don't love you." Carl's shoulders slumped. "You have to be realistic. I am the beautiful daughter of a wealthy landowner. I am destined to marry a very rich and powerful man like my father. You are a private in the Yankee army with questionable breeding. It cannot be, my darling."

Carl looked down at his feet, "Is there no way?"

"Go back to your northern sweetheart, Carl. You're a good man, and you deserve someone who loves you as much she does."

Chapter Eleven: The Arrest

A distant booming interrupted the farewells. "Those are cannons," Kyle said, turning his eyes upriver.

"We must have started the assault," Carl said.

"It's time for us to go," Kathryn said hurriedly.

"Listen," Kyle said, "stay off the main road. Swing wide to the west before you circle back to your own troops north of the city."

"Okay," Carl said, flinching at the sounds of cannon.

"And don't forget to change uniforms when you get close to your own," Liza said.

"Oh boy, I almost forgot what I'm wearing!" Carl said, looking down at the gray uniform he had on.

"Don't worry," Elijah said, "I'll remind him."

"Now you're really in trouble," Liza said flatly.

After a last round of farewells, Kyle mounted his horse and led the two women in the wagon back to the plantation. Carl and Elijah watched them until they disappeared from sight. Snowflakes swirled in the morning light as they left their hiding spot and crossed the road that ran between New Madrid and Point Pleasant. Carl stole a glance back towards town. Men in gray were riding hard towards them.

"Oh, shit!" Carl hissed. "Get on!" he called to Elijah extending his hand.

"I'm too big, sir! She can't carry us both," Elijah said, "Run, sir! I'll slow them down."

"Damn it, I can't leave you now!" Carl leaped from his horse. "Come on!" he shouted as he led his horse by the reigns into the brush on the other side of the road. They ran for the tree line across the muddy field before them. Carl stole a glance at the gray riders. They too had cut to the west and were now riding parallel to them. Panic surged through him. There was no way they could outrun cavalry. He fought the instinct to jump on his horse and leave Elijah to his fate, but he knew he wouldn't get far anyway, and then he would have to face the shame of his own cowardice.

They pressed hard into the woods, still pushing west, hoping to lose them in the trees. The gray-clad horsemen came exploding into their field of vision. Soon they were surrounded by a dozen or so men with sabers and pistols pointing at them. Elijah and Carl put their hands up.

A cold laugh broke the brief silence. Lieutenant Lathan Woods hopped off his horse. "On your knees," he said. The two knelt down carefully still keeping their hands in the air. Carl let go of his horse's reigns. "Cousin Carl!" Lathan smiled, "Looks like we'll be hanging you as a spy." Lathan's men chuckled grimly. "And you, big fella," Lathan squatted to look Elijah in the eye, "striking a white man is certainly a flogging offense, if not a capital one." He grinned at Elijah's obvious fear. "But a big, horse talking negro like yourself is too valuable to kill." Elijah betrayed a bit of relief. "But I think this is the second time I've caught you running. There ain't going to be a third." Lathan stood, "We're going to have to take one of them legs now before someone back in town tries to talk me out of it."

"What?!" Carl shouted.

Lathan slapped him hard across the face, "Be happy we don't take a limb from you too, but we'll need that extra weight to hang you." Lathan's men laughed darkly. "Hold them down!" He barked at his men.

Elijah punched the first man to approach him. It took several men to wrestle him to the ground. One of them tore Elijah's pant leg up to the thigh. Another cinched a belt around Elijah's leg, just above the knee. "Nice and tight, Dave," Lathan said. The man he called Dave went back to his horse and pulled a saw from his saddle bag.

"No!" Carl screamed. One of the men holding him punched him in the stomach, doubling him over. "Please, God, no…" Carl gasped for air.

The man called Dave pressed the saw to the bare flesh around Elijah's knee. "Now hold him still. He's an ornery one," he said. Carl heard a loud crack. Dave fell back to the ground and stared lifelessly at the sky. A perfect hole in his forehead started to bleed.

"Sharpshooter!" one of the men cried. Another crack rang out, dropping one of the men holding Carl.

"Horses!" another man called out. Carl could see blue men on horseback with sabers out charging Lathan's squad of Rebels.

"There's too many of them!" another man shouted, before falling to the ground with a hole in his head. The rest of the Rebels dashed off on their horses leaving Elijah and Carl behind. Soon the two were surrounded by Federal horsemen who pointed their pistols and sabers at them.

Carl put his hands up and then looked down at his gray uniform. "Wait...I can explain..." Carl stammered but fell silent as a man in an immaculate officer's uniform walked out into the circle of horsemen. Tinted spectacles concealed his eyes. His left hand had been replaced by a brass claw that was clamped onto the barrel of a rifle that had a long brass sight mounted on it. The man placed the butt of the rifle on the ground and then pulled a lever on his left forearm releasing the rifle from his claw. With his remaining right hand, he pulled off his tinted glasses and glared at Carl.

"Klaus...?" Carl gasped. "My God, I never thought I'd be so happy to see you!"

"Arrest that man," Klaus said flatly. Two men leaped from their horses and laid their hands on Carl.

"Wait a minute! I can explain!" Carl protested.

"Save it for your court-martial," Klaus said.

"Court-martial?!" Carl spewed

"It's a pity," Klaus allowed a slight smile, "I was hoping to extract satisfaction from you myself. Seems I'll have to be content watching your firing squad." Klaus looked to the men holding Carl, "Take him back to camp."

"Yes, lieutenant," the men replied, curtly leading Carl away.

"Lieutenant?! How is it that everyone outranks me in this stupid war?!" Carl cried out as they took him away.

Carl lay on the floor of the makeshift stockade, beat up and broken hearted. He had lost track of the time he spent there but knew it had been days. In the confusion over his uniform, Klaus's men had put him with Rebel prisoners at the rear of a large Union column on its way to take Point Pleasant.

Colonel Plummer had marched a brigade south from the Union position at Sikeston to Point Pleasant taking a wide path to the west around New Madrid and the Confederate forces there. The column was 3,000 men strong and made up of infantry regiments from Missouri, and Illinois, along with Wisconsin artillery and Michigan cavalry.

Carl hid his face in shame every time he saw a fellow trooper ride by. He hoped none of his comrades would recognize him as he walked along with fellow gray-clad men. His swollen black eye and unwashed face did much to hide him. Mercifully, his fellow prisoners didn't talk much. Each man stared downward in his own dejected misery as they marched behind the Union column.

He spent a cold night huddled with the other prisoners as light snow collected on their shivering bodies. At dawn, the Federal guns opened fire at the two Confederate transports docked at Point Pleasant for refueling. The ships scurried away, ridden with bullets and shell fragments. With little resistance, the Federals took the town of Pleasant Point. They immediately began to dig gun emplacements and trenches along the river. The Rebels sent gunboats over to try to dislodge them, but the Federals repelled them each time with rifle and cannon fire. Eventually, the Confederates took up positions on the other side over the river. Both sides settled into a stalemate of exchanging cannon fire, with little effect, that lasted for days.

With the town secured, the Federals began to process the prisoners. Most were slated to be shipped to prison camps in the North, but Carl was an exception. Once identified, he was separated from the rest until they could decide what to do with him. Desertion and treason were the words Carl heard being tossed around as officers discussed his fate. So Carl was locked in an empty room in a deserted townhouse and placed under guard. There he lay for days staring at the ceiling feeling sorry for himself. He tried to pull Kathryn's face into his mind, but the image was already fading and morphing into something that was a mix between her and Anna. Then Carl thought of his mother and the shame she would feel once she heard the news that her son had been shot as a deserter. He cried softly to himself trying not to be heard by the guards outside his room.

Carl woke to a key rattling the lock on his door. The morning sun was beaming through the window. The tears from the night before had become crust that he tried to rub away as the doorknob turned. In walked a tall, handsome man in a captain's uniform and a bold bushy mustache. Carl rubbed and squinted his blackened eye to make out the form of Captain Chester Newman. Newman towered over him with his hands on his hips, then broke the silence with a hearty laugh.

"Get me some chairs!" Newman called over his shoulder. "We're not going to sit on the floor like some damn savages!" An orderly brought in chairs. Newman sat in one and gestured to Carl to take the other. Carl dragged himself off the floor and slumped into the chair across from his company commander. Shame made it nearly impossible for Carl to meet his eyes, so he gazed at nothing on the floor.

"Good God, son, you look terrible," Newman said, "and you stink too." Carl sunk into his shame staring at the ground. Newman looked over at the tray of uneaten food on the floor next to the door. "Son, you have to eat. We'll get you cleaned up too, but you have to talk to me. Right now, it doesn't look so good. You go missing and then turn up in the enemy's uniform. I have done all I can to keep them from stringing you up. They're talking hanging, firing squads, flogging, branding…all sorts of terrible things." Newman paused to see if his words were breaking through Carl's dejected silence.

"Now listen," Newman continued, "you are one of my boys. I brought you here, and damn it, if it's in my power, I will bring you home when this is all said and done. But you have got to help me. Tell me the truth, all of it. I swear, if I think you're lying to me, I will blacken that other eye."

Carl let out a sigh and then looked up into Newman's eyes. He saw hope. He told him everything. He told him how he got lost chasing the Rebel cavalryman, how he was jumped by a man that turned out to be his friend, how they went back to Kyle's plantation because it was too late and dark to find his way back to base. He told him how he agreed to help them get their slave back and the adventure in New Madrid.

Newman listened intently, his hand stroking his mustache as the story got crazier and crazier. He seemed to be trying to control himself from interrupting with, "Bullshit!" But the mention of New Madrid and the forts inside caused his eyebrows to pop up out of their scowl.

"You've been to New Madrid?" he asked.

"Yes, sir," Carl replied.

"You've been inside both forts there?"

"Fort Thompson and Fort Bankhead, yes, sir," he answered.

"Do you think you could describe them, draw diagrams, tell us how they're laid out?"

"I suppose I could…" Carl said looking up at this Captain.

"Bully!" Newman leaped from his chair knocking it over in the process. "Don't go anywhere! I'll be right back!"

Within ten minutes, a guard brought a washbowl full of warm water, soap, rags, and Carl's blue uniform. A sergeant came a half hour later with two armed guards. "Come with me," he said curtly, as he led Carl out of the darkness of the house into the sunlight.

General Pope stared out the window. His back was turned to a room full of subordinate generals who had come for the council of war. They were in the parlor of one of the houses commandeered by Federal forces at Point Pleasant. It was where Pope made his headquarters. Pope watched the ongoings outside: the marching, the moving of supplies, the fortifying of earthen works; all while the distant thunder continued as Flag Officer Foote's fleet traded shells with the batteries on Island No. Ten.

That Federal brown-water flotilla stayed cautiously north of the first bend in the river. Foote insisted that Island No. 10 was too well armed to try to push past it in order to clear the Confederate gunboats moored outside of New Madrid, which was on the second bend in the river. Foote and his boats had taken quite a beating at Fort Donelson. Foote himself had been wounded in the battle, ironically enough, in the foot. This reluctance caused Pope's plans to take New Madrid and Island No. 10 to stall. Pope felt he couldn't take either until the Rebel gunboats were cleared from the river by Foote's ironclad flotilla. Foote felt he couldn't take the gunboats until the batteries on the island and along the shores were cleared out by the army. So they sat in a tactical stalemate, and time was running out.

"Gentlemen," Pope started, still peering out the window, "if we don't move on New Madrid soon, we will lose all that we have worked for." General Pope turned around to face his officers. "Our overall commander, Major General Halleck, is aware of Flag Officer Foote's reluctance to engage, thus putting us at peril with the Confederate gunboats. In lieu of naval support, I have asked for an additional 30,000 troops to take New Madrid and to destroy the Rebel ships from the shores. General Halleck has declined.

Instead, he's suggesting we abandon our goals here, and instead, hand over our command to General Smith, who is now working his way down the Tennessee River to attack the Rebel stronghold at Corinth in Mississippi."

That got a round of scoffs and moans from the men gathered in the room. General Pope searched the eyes of the men around him. "I suggest we attack New Madrid at first opportunity before we are forced to admit defeat."

"But sir," one of the brigade commanders interjected, "we don't know the enemy's strength at New Madrid, nor his gun placements. We could be marching into a slaughter!"

"...And even if we do take the town," another piped in, "without heavy artillery, we'll be no match for the Rebel ships. They will shell us with impunity."

"I've ordered siege guns to be sent here. Hopefully, they'll arrive in time for the assault. As for what lies beyond the earthen works that surround the town, we do have some intelligence on their strength and gun placements."

"I'd hardly trust the word of Rebel captives," one of the officers scoffed, "they inflate their numbers to match their egos. The deserters do just the opposite. We can't trust either of them."

"We may have had some of our own eyes on the inside," Pope said, and then turned his eyes to his old friend, "Colonel Granger, are they here?"

"Yes, of course!" Granger sat up in his chair stroking his beard. He gave a nod to one of his aides who stood alongside the wall behind the row of seated officers. The young man scurried out of the room. Moments later, a tall, handsome man with a heavy mustache walked in wearing an immaculate captain's uniform, his captain's hat tucked under his arm. Behind him came a nervous-looking private with a swollen shut-eye and a mess of black hair. His one open green eye scanned the room of high ranking officers. General Pope and Colonel Granger regarded the private with surprise.

"This is the man who's been behind the lines at New Madrid?" Pope cocked an eyebrow.

"Yes, sir!" Captain Newman replied. "This is Private Carl Smith. He's also been inside Fort Thompson and Fort Bankhead that defend the city on either side."

"I hear you're a deserter," Pope scrutinized Carl from head to toe.

"No, sir, I was captured after chasing enemy cavalry…sir…" Carl answered.

Pope paused a moment, staring at Carl. Carl felt the whole room staring at him. "How well can you describe the forts and the city, son? Do you think you could draw out diagrams of where their guns are placed?" Pope asked at last.

"Yes, sir, fairly so, I believe," Carl answered, his one good eye scanning the room.

"You say you're not a deserter?" Pope asked again.

"No, sir!" Carl said, more confidently than before.

"And you're not a coward?" Pope asked.

"I don't think I am…sir," Carl said.

"I see…" Pope said, eyeing Carl as if he were trying to read his very soul. "We shall test that. I want you first over the ramparts when we make our assault." Carl tried not to flinch at the thought of running head first into the enemy's fire. "In the meantime, you will give a full account of everything you've seen inside. You will assist us in our planning to your full ability. Do you understand?"

"Yes, sir, I do," Carl said. Pope and Granger continued to eye Carl as if trying to solve a riddle. "Um…what is it…sir?"

Pope exchanged a glance with Colonel Granger and then back to Carl. "You remind me of someone I once knew during the Mexican war."

"My father, Lieutenant David Smith, fought in the war," Carl offered.

"The man I'm thinking of didn't fight for us…" General Pope said softly, his eyes somewhere far away. Carl cocked an eyebrow in confusion. Pope then focused his eyes on something outside, "They're here!" Pope moved quickly to the window as other officers started rising from their chairs. "Gentlemen, our heavy artillery is arriving at this very moment. Colonel Granger, I want you and your staff to debrief Private Smith. I want a full report on my desk in two hours. Gentlemen, we will take New Madrid in short order!"

A cheer broke out in the room. Carl could only think about having to be the first over the ramparts. Captain Newman read him well and put his arm around Carl's slumped shoulders. "Cheer up, son! At least it'll be one of their bullets and not one from our firing squad that does you in," he chuckled. Carl didn't think it was funny.

Chapter Twelve: The Battle for New Madrid

The Federals went to work immediately with the arrival of their heavy siege guns. General Pope was confident that the newly arrived 24-pounders and 8-inch howitzers would do the work Flag Officer Foote and his fleet refused to do. Once in place, Pope's new guns would pound the enemy forts that straddled the town and the gunboats on the river into submission. New Madrid would be his and Island No. 10 would fall soon after.

Crews spent the afternoon digging gun placements for the heavy cannons and trenches for the supporting riflemen; all of this taking place within 800 yards of Fort Thompson's earthen walls. The Confederates' forward picket line was closer still. With Rebel sharpshooters just 150 yards away, the work was dangerous. Regiments, therefore, took turns digging or standing guard over the men with shovels, returning fire when Rebels played target practice on the toiling men.

Lieutenant Klaus Schmidt took particular joy in handing out retribution to any Confederate who thought himself handy with a rifle. Despite the loss of his left hand, Klaus's family connection assured him the lieutenant commission he had planned for. Already a known marksman, Klaus spent much of his time training with the sharpshooter regiments until the army decided what to do with the one-handed lieutenant. Eventually, he was assigned as an aide to

Colonel Granger who commanded the 2nd and 3rd Michigan Volunteer Cavalry regiments.

Not content with merely waiting for orders from the gruff commander, Klaus made himself busy by leading patrols, organizing vedettes, and training men as sharpshooters.

"There," Klaus whispered to one of the pickets he had placed in the wood line. "Do you see the wisp of smoke at about 150 yards?"

"Barely," the riflemen said.

"That's a man smoking a pipe. He's been taking poorly aimed shots at our men all afternoon. When I give you the signal, I want you to raise your hat on this stick," Klaus told the man.

"Um, okay, if you say so, sir."

"Good," Klaus whispered and patted the confused man on the shoulder with his brass claw. He then drew back into the woods. Moments later, he reappeared 50 yards to the man's right, taking cover behind a tree. With his rifle clinched in his claw, he motioned with his one good hand for the man to raise his hat. The blue kepi hat slowly rose above the brush into plain view. The distant wisp of smoke broke apart as a man in gray popped up with his rifle to take aim.

CRACK!

The man fell back with a spray of blood before he could even fire off a shot. A round of cheers broke along the Federal line. "Maybe that will teach them a bit of caution," Klaus said to no one in particular.

Klaus's shot did nothing to stop the Rebel harassment. Confederate cannons and rifles picked away at the Federals all afternoon and into the evening. Not everyone was impressed with their marksmanship. Having finished debriefing Carl about the gun placements at Fort Thompson, Colonel Granger walked along the line of heavy siege guns, personally setting the aim and elevation of some of them. He did this all while Rebel cannonballs crashed into the earthworks, showering him and his retinue with dirt. The men around him flinched and ducked, but Granger seemed to not take any notice of the danger, only merely dusting off the dirt flung onto his uniform from time to time with dispassionate contempt.

Not every man's disregard for the dangers went unpunished. The Rebel guns mostly quieted as night fell, but the sharpshooters still took delight in taking occasional shots when targets presented themselves. Captain Carr of the 10th Illinois used the cover of night to inspect his forward pickets. He crouched low and shuffled out to one of the rifle pits with his unlit pipe clutched between his teeth. The pair of soldiers tucked in there for the night watch looked up at him as he approached.

"You boys see any movement so far?" the captain said in a low voice.

"No, sir. They've been pretty quiet since nightfall," one of the men replied.

"Well, don't let your guard down," the captain said, striking a match to relight his pipe. "They're still out there and they're watching us just close…"

CRACK!

"Good God!" he cried as a Minié ball found him in the darkness.

"Ha, ha!" a Southern voice called from a distance, "did that hurt ya any?"

The captain turned to run back to the Federal line when a second ball dropped him where he stood.

The Federal work on the gun placements and rifle trenches continued into the night. After a few hard lessons, like the death of Captain Carr, men were extremely careful not to make themselves easy targets. The only lights to be seen were the gleaming arcs that cut across the sky as Flag Officer Foote's ironclad flotilla continued its bombardment of Island No. 10, some 12 miles away.

By three in the morning, the guns were ready. At dawn, they opened fire. The effects were almost immediate. One of the Federal shells struck a 32-pounder at Fort Thompson killing two Rebel gunners and wounding a third. Federal shells rained down on Fort Bankhead too, wrecking two of the guns there. Federal gunners directed their fire at Rebel gunboats as well. The CSS Mohawk was steaming its way into action with General McCown and his staff on board when a shell smashed into the pilothouse and ripped off both legs of his chief medical officer, spraying the other men with gore.

"Good God!" McCown gasped, as he wiped the splattered blood from his eyes.

The Rebel gunners started finding their own targets once the fog lifted around nine that morning, sometimes even picking up spent Federal balls and firing them back. One shot hit a Union 24-pounder directly on the muzzle instantly killing its gunner and wounding six men near it.

By ten in the morning, a division of Federal troops marched around the city's flank to attack Fort Bankhead on the other side of town. The blue troops formed up in the tree line, 800 yards from the Fort. But before they could launch an attack, concentrated fire from the Rebel gunboats sent the Federals tumbling back for cover.

The dueling cannonades continued through the day, tapering off at times, and then reigniting with new fury. Cannonballs bounded across the flat ground between the two armies. Some buried themselves in the earthworks in front of the trenches, showering men with dirt. Some dropped into trenches on a lucky hop and mangled the men inside as the shots ricocheted off the walls.

The guns began to quiet as darkness poured in. The sounds of cannons were soon replaced with peals thunder. Thick, black clouds rolled in and blotted out the sky. Carl huddled in a trench with his new found companions. Instead of returning to his comrades in the 2nd Michigan Cavalry, Carl was placed with several companies of the US 1st Infantry. They were designated to be the first over the earthen walls of Fort Thompson when the assault would begin. Carl, with his inside experience of the fort, was there to assist and advise Captain Mower, the man who would lead the assault.

Carl didn't make too many friends with the US Regulars. The men of the 1st Infantry regarded him with much suspicion. He was an outsider, an "uppity" cavalryman, and quite possibly, a deserter. That suited Carl just fine. That and the raging battle kept most of the questions and conversation to a minimum. Most of the day, they watched the artillery duel from their trenches, ducking often as shells and cannon balls came screaming overhead. Still, some men were curious about his Colt revolving carbine that seemed so alien compared to their big Springfield rifles.

"Where do ya put the bayonet?" a man asked.

"There isn't one. We don't use them on horseback," Carl answered.

"Then how ya' gonna stick 'em when we go over the wall?" another man asked.

"I suppose I'll use my sword," Carl said, realizing he hadn't quite imagined what he'd be doing as they attacked the fort on foot.

A third man with sergeant stripes took a pipe out of his mouth and pointed it at Carl, "Then how ya gonna shoot?"

"Well, I've got a pistol for my other hand," Carl said.

"Hmm," the pipe-smoking sergeant said, "sounds like you're going to run out of hands."

Fat raindrops mercifully stopped the men's needling. Soon torrents of rain forced the men to cower under their blankets, great coats, or anything else they had that might protect them from the downpour, but little did. The men were soaked before long, standing in deep pools as the trenches began to fill with muddy water.

Through the hiss of rain, the men could hear the churning of steam engines on the river. Each flash of lighting revealed large troop transports coming and going to the two forts along the river that bookended the town. "They're reinforcing," said the sergeant, as he cleaned out the soaked ashes in his pipe with his pinky, "we're in for a fight tomorrow, boys."

Carl didn't want to think about it. After a day of watching the enormous amount of cannon balls bounding across the way, he couldn't imagine running directly into them. How could he expect to survive? Would he die instantly, or be one of those ruined men screeching in agony on the ground? He felt for his locket that held Anna's picture under his shell jacket but decided to leave it there as the rain might ruin it. So he snuggled in, using his blanket like a cocoon, with his cap sealing off the top, and tried to picture Kathryn's face in his mind.

"Hey!" a voice hissed as someone nudged him. "Wake up, we're fixing to go over the wall." Carl peered through the small gap between his cap and the blanket. The sergeant was pointing at him with his pipe. "Better get your weapons ready." Carl blinked at him and looked down the row of men in the trench.

They were smoking, ramrodding their rifles, and placing primers on the nipples. Carl slowly unwrapped himself, his muscles stiff from sleeping in the damp cold. Someone handed him a hot cup of coffee, which he accepted gratefully. Across the field, he could see drifting patches of fog lingering between them and the silent fort.

He then pulled out his pistol, checking to make sure the cylinders were loaded and each nipple had a percussion cap. Then he checked his revolving carbine.

"Must be nice to have all those fancy guns," the man next to him said, "I have to reload each time I shoot!"

Carl shrugged. "It'd be better if I didn't need to use them at all," he said, checking his saber next to see if it still held an edge. *Everything is just how it was the 20 times I checked yesterday,* he thought to himself.

"Get ready to go over the top!" Captain Mower called out to the men as he made his way to the center of the trench where Carl was. Sergeants repeated the order along the line. "Are you ready, son?" Mower put a hand on Carl's shoulder.

"I guess so, sir," Carl said. This was it, he realized. Everything he was, everything he had hoped to be would be ended by a cannonball, a bullet, or a shell fragment fired by a man he would never see, by a man who would never know anything about him. He was sick to his stomach. The fear and sense of loss brought bile to his mouth.

"According to your diagram, that spot there lies between two batteries," the captain pointed to the crudely drawn map and then to the imposing earthen walls of Fort Thompson across the way. He looked at Carl's whitened face. "Good Lord, son, pull yourself together!" Carl vomited out the coffee and the little hardtack he had in his stomach. Captain Mower had to leap out of the way to avoid getting it on his boots. The men around broke into a nervous laugh.

"I'm sorry, sir," Carl said, wiping the string of saliva that hung from his mouth with his sleeve.

Captain Mower looked at him for a moment and then gave him a soft smile, "If this is our last moment, let's put on a good show."

Carl returned the smile weakly.

"Here you go, son," the pipe-smoking sergeant handed Carl a clear glass bottle full of golden brown liquid, "take some courage and pass it around." Carl took a hard pull from the bottle. The liquid tasted like earthy grains and burned like fire as it slid down his throat. He shuddered, bringing his fist to mouth to keep from retching it back out. The men around him burst into laughter again. Carl handed the bottle to the next man and let out a sigh. Some of the tension released, and for a moment, he felt at peace.

"You ready, son?" Mower asked once again.

"Fuck it, let's go," Carl said.

Captain Mower pulled out his sword, "You heard the man, 'Fuck it, let's go!'" The men laughed and let out a cheer as they poured over the top of the trench into the field before them. Carl climbed over the top expecting to be shot immediately. When it didn't happen right away he realized he had his eyes clenched tight. He opened them as he stumbled forward. He quickly caught his balance and shuffled forward to stay close to Captain Mower, who was marching forward holding his saber straight out to point to their intended destination: the enemy walls of Fort Thompson.

"Hold the line! Tighten up!" sergeants yelled, as they ran up and down the line of men marching forward across the mushy, cannon-scarred field.

Carl could hear the squish of hundreds of men tramping on wet ground. Still, no sounds of fire came from the Rebels. "They must be waiting until we get close; that's what I'd do," a man said to one of his neighbors.

"Keep quiet and hold the line," a sergeant barked. "Watch for rifles to pop up over the wall!"

Carl could make out the tops of two rifles pointing up from the wall. Still, no gunshots came. Carl wrung his carbine nervously. *They must be waiting until they can't miss!*

With no immediate gunfire to contend with, Mower called out to fix bayonets. Sergeants repeated the order along the line of marching men. Carl heard the rattle and clicks as two hundred men pulled bayonets from their sheaths and locked them into place at the end of their barrels. Carl gripped his carbine tight realizing he didn't have enough arms to also pull out his sword.

"At the double!" Captain Mower called out. The sergeants repeated and the men broke into a steady jog towards the looming earthen wall. The squishing of their feet in the soggy ground grew louder. Still, no shots came from the Confederates.

This is crazy! Carl thought.

The men slowed their pace as they approached the wall until they simply stopped at the foot of it in confusion. Men looked at each other and shrugged. "Now what?" some of them said.

Mower turned to Carl, "Well, son, this your show. Climb over and tell us what's going on."

Carl blinked at him blankly and then looked up at the six-foot wall. "…What…?"

"Come on boys!" the sergeant with the pipe called out to some of the men, "Let's help him over!" Men squatted with their backs to the wall cupping their hands and lacing their fingers together to give Carl a foothold. "Come on, son," he beaconed with his hand, "let's go!"

Carl shrugged and then put his foot into the soldiers' hands. They hoisted him up slowly. "Hold up!" Carl hissed as his eyes crested the top. There was no one there. Carl scanned the fort quickly, sure that a bullet would catch him between the eyes as he looked for signs of life. There were none.

"Higher!" he hissed down at the men. He planted his Colt revolving carbine on the top of the wall and hoisted himself up and over, jumping down to the ground with a thud. He was sure that would alert the enemy of his presence. He snapped the butt of his carbine to his shoulder quickly scanning for targets. There were none.

To his left, he saw the two rifles he had seen during the approach. They were leaning against the wall. Laying on the ground next to them were two gray-clad bodies. Carl approached them slowly clutching his carbine and constantly scanning all around him for an imminent attack. He got close to the two slumped bodies on the ground, did a quick scan, and then slowly extended the muzzle of his carbine to push one of the bodies over to see its wounds. He was wary of what he might see.

Instead of rolling over, the body sat up and rubbed its eyes, causing Carl to leap back in terror. He looked up at Carl with big, blue, sleepy eyes. He had a mop of straw-colored hair and a chubby face marked by sleeping on the sleeve of his jacket. He wiped a line of drool that was making its way down his dirty face with that same sleeve.

"Oh, is it time to go?" he asked Carl.

His brown-haired companion sat up and blinked at Carl in confusion as well. Both of them seemed to be barely teenagers. "Wait...you're one of them..." he said, rubbing his eyes.

"Dang it!" the blond-haired boy said, "we done missed the last transport! They left us!"

"I guess we shouldn't've fall'n asleep," the second boy said, scratching his head.

"We were supposed to be watching for you Yankees while they were loading the boats," the first one said. "I guess they done forgot to come get us before the last one left."

"Yup, looks like it!" the second shook his head.

"Well, ain't that something!" the first boy said, "I guess we'll have to go with you then, sir."

"Yup, looks like it!" the second boy said again.

"Hey, what time do you guys serve breakfast? I sure am hungry!" the blond-headed kid said with enthusiasm.

"Heck yeah! I hear you Yankees got all the good food!" the second boy said with excitement.

"Hey!" the sergeant yelled from the other side of the wall, "what the hell is going on over there?!"

The two boys' eyes bulged with fear, "They ain't gonna treat us bad, are they, Mister?" the blond boy asked.

"I don't know," Carl said, "they're not too crazy about me either."

Chapter Thirteen: Unfinished Business

"Hey!" the sergeant yelled again.

"It's all clear!" Carl yelled back. "They're all gone except for two...and they've surrendered!" Carl then turned back to the two boys in gray uniforms. "Quickly, do you know a Lieutenant Bethune, Kyle Bethune?" he asked, nervously looking over his shoulder as the blue men came pouring over the wall.

"Why, yes!" said the blond-headed boy. "He was holler'n all night on his horse, trying to get the supplies and everyone on the transports. I reckon he must've got on one himself at the end. I don't know who was supposed to come and get us..." Carl felt relieved. Kyle had survived the barrage and got away.

"What do we have here?" the pipe-smoking sergeant came up behind Carl.

"These two are what's left of the rear guard, Sergeant. They surrendered peacefully," Carl said. The two boys looked up at the sergeant doe-eyed.

"Alright, boys, come with me," the sergeant said.

"When do we get to eat?" the brown-haired boy asked.

"I sure am hungry!" the blond added.

"I'm sure we'll find you something," the sergeant said as he led them away.

The Rebels had left the fort in a hurry. Evidence of a hasty retreat was everywhere. The dead had been left where they had fallen. Half eaten food sat on plates. Candles still burned in some of the tents. The Federals found boxes of discarded supplies and ammunition, some of which had to be fished out of the river. The Rebels had tried to disable their heavy siege guns by driving spikes into the touch holes, but these were easily removed leaving the Federals with a bounty of large guns and supplies.

The town looked very different from when Carl had been there last, a little more than a week before. The Confederates had burned houses to the ground and chopped down trees to give their guns a clear range of fire. The Rebels were now gone, but they had not gone far. General McCown had concentrated his troops upstream at Island No.10, and among the shore batteries that lined the Tennessee side of the river. Gunboats and mortar rafts clustered there as well, to create the last defense of the Mississippi north of Fort Pillow and Memphis.

General Pope's plan was to bring his army across the river and attack the Rebels that taunted them from the Tennessee side, but he needed Flag Officer Foote's ironclad ships to cover the crossing. Otherwise, the Confederate gunboats would easily blast his Army to pieces as they tried to get to the other side of the river.

Foote wouldn't budge. He and his ships had taken a beating at Donelson. Foote himself was injured and commanded his fleet from a pair of crutches; he wasn't about to risk his ships in another direct assault on a well-fortified position. So he held his fleet just north of the island, hiding out of sight around the bend of the river. From there he was content to lob shells at the Rebels at a safe distance with little effect.

This stalemate also cut off the flow of supplies to the Federals by way of the river. If Federal boats couldn't get past Island No. 10, General Pope would have to find another way. He decided to dig his way around the island.

The Mississippi was shaped like a winding snake at the place where it separated the states of Kentucky and Tennessee on the east side, from Missouri on the west. The river flowed south to Island No. 10, then took a 180° turn to flow north for nine miles to New Madrid. There it took another 180° turn and continued its path south. The two large bends in the river created a large "S" shape laying on its front side as one would view it on a map.

By digging a canal through miles of flooded woods and fields, the Federals could connect the Saint James Bayou, which broke off to the west from the Mississippi River north of the island, to the Saint John Bayou, that flowed back into the river at New Madrid. For two weeks, a force of engineers toiled to clear the way for steamboats by digging and removing tree stumps in the way.

Having done his part in taking New Madrid, Carl was allowed to return to his cavalry unit, although the reception from his fellow troopers was less than welcoming. "Well, look who's here, it's the deserter," Private Max Bates spit on the ground.

"I heard he's a traitor," his nearby companion chimed in, "caught in an enemy uniform, even." Men stood up from their campfires and circled around, eager to be entertained by the imminent confrontation. Carl scanned the sneering faces looking for friends. He found none. Hans and Dieter were among them standing to Carl's right. Their folded arms revealed two golden stripes sewn onto their uniforms.

"You guys are corporals now?!" Carl gasped in indignation. The two Germans blinked at him impassively, then flinched in surprise. Carl caught a glimpse of a fist coming to his left. He had just enough time to cringe and pull his hands to the sides of his head to soften the blow.

Bates' right hook sent him tumbling to the ground. The men gave out a cheer as the promise of entertainment proved to be true. Rough hands pulled him off the ground and shoved him into the waiting Bates who met him with a blow to the stomach. Carl doubled over from the blow but used the momentum of the shove to drive his shoulder into Bates' midsection. The two went down with Carl's arms wrapped around Bates' waist. Bates went straight onto his back with an "oof!" as the air ejected from his lungs. Carl scrambled to mount the stunned and supine Bates, drawing his fist back to pound his face. Hands from behind grabbed his fist. Then several were pulling Carl off the helpless man.

"Goddamnit!" Sergeant Barth barked, "You're not back two minutes and you're already trouble!" Barth then looked over at Bates who was being helped up. "I ought to get a horse whip and lick the fight out of ya!" Sergeant Barth turned to glare at all the men in the circle. The men dared not to meet his eyes, instead, most of them looked to the ground, some pawing it with their feet. "But we don't have time for that. Get to your horses. We're going on patrol, and you two…"

Carl and Bates looked up at the red-faced sergeant. "Are we done here, or do you need to cool off in the stockade?"

Carl looked at Bates and then back to Sergeant Barth, "We're done, Sergeant." Bates continued to look down.

"Bates!" Barth shouted.

"We're done," he mumbled.

"Get your gear and your horses. We're heading out in ten minutes," Sergeant Barth said and stormed off.

Carl looked at Bates, "I didn't desert, Max. I'm no traitor."

Bates looked up at him and then walked away, "We'll see."

The stables were a busy place. Men were returning from duty while others were saddling up to go out on patrol or to man the vedettes. For the first time in over a week, Carl found a reason to smile in all that chaos. Among the shuffling soldiers with their horses and the stablehands attending them, was a large black man helping a trooper onto his saddle. Relief and happiness washed over Carl as he recognized the first friendly face he'd seen in weeks.

"Elijah, you live!" Carl called out. Elijah's big, brown eyes softened as he recognized Carl.

"Mr. Carl, I thought they was gonna kill you!" Elijah boomed in joy.

"Me too!" Carl said, slapping Elijah's arm, "I see you've found a place here."

"Yes, sir," Elijah beamed, "and they even pay me. I'm a free man!"

"I'm so happy for you, Elijah," Carl said looking at his soft eyes.

"I wish I could do more," Elijah said, "they talking about letting us color folk do some of the fighting too."

"Well, I hope this is all over before anyone gets the chance to take a shot at you. You're just too big of a target!" Carl said, squeezing Elijah's hands.

Elijah dropped his eyes to his hands shyly and chuckled, "I suppose so." He lifted his eyes back to Carl's with excitement, "I've got Bessie all ready for you! I've been taking special care of her, sir!"

"Thank you. You don't have to call me 'sir' or 'mister,' I'm just Carl."

"I know, si…Carl. It's a hard habit to lose," Elijah said sheepishly.

Carl was grateful for the patrols and vedette duty that filled the days that followed. It meant he didn't have to talk or explain himself to anyone. Chucky was the only one interested in friendly conversation. Carl felt bad for discouraging it, but he didn't want to accidentally reveal what had really happened during his time away or his friendship with some of the people on the other side of the river.

Most of Carl's patrols were through the wetlands to protect the men digging the canal. He also spent long hours guarding roads, watching for any enemy movement on the Federal position at New Madrid. During his off time, Carl, like many of the bored soldiers, would find a spot along the river and watch the on-going artillery duel between the Federal boats and the Rebel batteries. Mortars arched across the sky and then plummeted to the earth. A cheer broke out among the men every time one managed to hit something on the rebel side or a gasp when one clanged against the metal armor of the Federal ships.

The *Eagle* was by far the most exciting spectacle for the men during that time. It seemed that life had come to a standstill as thousands of men stopped in their tracks and craned their necks to see large, spherical shape drift upward from the trees and into the sky above. The story passed among them that a German aeronaut named John Steiner had offered his services to Flag Officer Foote. In a wicker basket suspended from the hot air balloon, officers were able to observe the effects of their mortar rounds and then call down to the gunners to adjust their fire.

"The marvels of the modern world..." Sergeant Barth uttered in awe.

"Those fools are just asking to be shot down," Bates said, earning a murmured agreement from the men around him.

Carl looked at the men floating in the basket with awe and envy. *How far can they see? Can they see Kyle, the Bethune Plantation, Katherine?* he wondered, then shook his head as if to shoo away the thoughts of the redheaded beauty that crept in there.

The patrols and vedettes continued. Carl found himself going out at different times of the day and night with different groups, sometimes with just another man to guard a road, sometimes with a small squad of men through woods, and sometimes with his entire company. So it wasn't a surprise when he was awakened in the middle of the night to pull patrol duty.

"Hey!" a voice whispered, as a hand reached into his tent to shake his foot, "Get your gear, we're going on patrol." Thunder rumbled off in the distance.

Carl sat up and rubbed his eyes. He detected a faint German accent. "Dieter?"

"Ja, let's go!" the voice whispered back.

Carl shimmed into his trousers and swung the suspenders over his shoulders. He crawled out of his tent with his weapons, hat, and jacket. The night air was oddly warm. A strong gust of wind swirled campground litter along the rows of tents. The eerie glow of embers from campfires was the only source of light. Two dark figures stood waiting for him. Only a flash of lightning revealed Hans and Dieter's impassive faces. Carl looked around for more men, "Is it just you guys?"

"Ja, come on," Hans replied, turning on his heel. Carl looked around, then with a shrug, followed the two to the stables. Something wasn't right. Why would there be two corporals and one private on patrol?

Bess reared at a flash of lighting as Carl tried to mount her, "Easy, girl," he whispered, patting her on the neck. It seemed she too felt something was off, or perhaps it was just the coming storm. Many of the horses nickered and stomped their hooves as thunder rumbled and gusts of wind rattled the stables.

"Come," Dieter beaconed from his horse. Carl followed the two brothers into the woods. It was so dark he wondered how they were supposed to see anything, let alone the tree branches that lashed at him along the trail. Within moments of their ride into the woods, he could see a faint glow ahead that silhouetted the trees with a flicker.

"Hey! There's a light up ahead!" Carl hissed in a whisper.

"Good!" Dieter whispered. "Let's go there."

Thunder rumbled and Bess let out a snort of apprehension. Carl felt a wave of uneasiness spread over him. As they approached, the glow revealed itself to be a circle of torches staked into the ground in a small clearing of the woods.

"Let's dismount here and tie our horses," Dieter said.

Carl got off his horse full of reservation, "What is going on here?"

"You will see," Hans said mildly.

Carl let out a sigh as he began to realize the game at hand, "Should I bring my rifle?"

"Just your sword, please," Dieter replied, "you can leave your pistol with your horse as well...and any other encumberments."

Carl unfastened his pistol belt and removed his jacket. He pulled his saber from the scabbard mounted on his saddle and walked into the ring of torches. There stood a man waiting for him. The torchlight flickered off his brass claw.

"I see the army is very lenient with traitors," the man said.

"I'm no traitor, Klaus," Carl sighed.

"Unfortunately, we've been denied a court-martial to find out, certainly a lapse in justice for sure. Still, you and I have unfinished business, and in that, I offer you no lapse," Klaus said.

"You're a maniac, Klaus. Have you ever thought to ask your sister Anna what she wants?"

"The wants of a girl are inconsequential to the honor of a family. My sister will overcome her folly once she is married to a gentleman of stature. Until then, I will make sure she is unsullied by men of questionable lineage like you. Prepare to defend yourself." Klaus said, raising his saber and placing his brass claw on his rear hip.

Carl stepped forward with his right foot, raised his saber, and placed his left hand on his back hip as well. The two stepped forward and began to circle each other. The wind whipped through, rustling the leaves around their feet and threatened to blow out the torches. A flash of lightning prompted Klaus's attack. He charged forward with his saber held high and then brought it down swiftly towards Carl's head. Carl deflected the blow with his own saber, stepped to his right, and brought his blade around to attack Klaus's exposed belly. Klaus stopped it with his blade there and then buried his left foot into Carl's stomach, knocking him to the ground. Carl sat up quickly, clutching his saber as Klaus stepped forward with his own sword in hand. Strong wind whipped his hair around making it look like it was on fire with rage.

"You're not so lucky this time," Klaus smiled menacingly. At that moment, Carl heard a train coming.

That's funny, there're no tracks near here, he thought to himself. That's when he saw it, like some dark force ripping through the trees, swallowing up the light behind his looming enemy. "Klaus, look out!" he screamed.

"Hmmph!" Klaus smirked, "I'm not falling for your childish tricks!" That's when the wind picked him up and tossed him twenty feet away into the trees. Carl rolled over and pressed his face to the ground. All hell seemed to have broken loose around him. Sticks and debris pummeled him as he screamed in panic. The roar and fury were deafening. Then, just as quickly as it came, it was gone.

"What the hell was that?!" he yelled.

"It was a tornado. I think it just passed by us," Dieter said.

"Ja, we were definitely just outside of it," Hans added.

"Where's Klaus?" Carl asked, looking around frantically.

"There, come!" Dieter pointed to a clump of fallen trees. The three ran to the body sprawled on top of a pile of broken trees and branches. Klaus was still clutching his saber with his good hand. His claw was wedged in a notch in one of the fallen trees.

"Jesus Christ, are you okay?!" Carl blurted.

"Yes," Klaus said, shaking the fogginess from his head, "there's no need to blaspheme. Help me get my hand free."

The three wrestled to free his brass prosthetic from the tangle of branches. They could hear shouts and screams coming from the nearby camp. "Come," Klaus said now that he was free, "we must go!"

The tornado had torn a path through the Federal camp before crossing the river to wreak havoc among the Rebels. The four men broke out of the woods to witness a frantic scene. A tree had fallen across a tent. Men were trapped underneath screaming in pain.

"Come on!" Klaus yelled, slapping Carl on the back. The four ran to join a group of men forming around the tree.

"Hang on, down there! We'll get you out!" a man called to the men trapped below. "Come on now, boys!" he yelled to the handful of men around him, "Heave!"

The men put their backs into it, lifting the tree off the ground. Some of the trapped men were able to scurry out, others had to be pulled out, some were already dead.

Details about the tornado started to spread as the morning sunlight revealed the damage. Two privates and a lieutenant of the 7th Illinois Cavalry had been crushed to death by the tree. Seven others had been injured by the tornado. Some of the horses had died as well. Carl and his comrades didn't know how the Rebels on the other side of the river were affected, but they could clearly see one of the Confederate transports had been flipped over on the river. Its cabin was completely torn from the hull and now sat half submerged along the muddy Tennessee shore.

There was more overnight news that filled the men with excitement. After weeks of inactivity, Flag Officer Foote had ordered an overnight raid on one of the

Rebel batteries. Fifty sailors and 50 men from the 42nd Illinois loaded onto five longboats and rowed under the cover of darkness to a fortified gun placement on the Tennessee side. The only resistance there was a picket of two Rebel soldiers who hastily fired at the approaching Yankees and then ran off for help. The raiding party went to work driving spikes into the touch holes of all the cannons, disabling them from further use. The men then slipped back into their boats and rowed to safety before a Rebel force could come and confront them.

This brought much cheer and celebration on the Federal side of the river. The good news seemed to soften the tragedy of the tornado that had occurred after the raid. Men talked at length around their campfires about what the overnight raid meant. Most of them agreed that a full-on Federal attack was imminent.

Chapter Fourteen: A Tearful Goodbye

After weeks of General Pope's pleading, the War Department's prodding, and the general haranguing from the Northern press, Flag Officer Foote decided to move. The canal dug by the Federals allowed for much-needed supplies to reach Pope's forces at New Madrid but proved to be too shallow for the ironclad gunboats to pass through. So Foote would finally send two ironclad gunships through the gauntlet of Island No.10's batteries.

Commander Henry Walke, captain of the *Carondelet*, volunteered her and her 14 guns to make the first run. She would have to run straight at the island, coming within 300 yards of its guns before she could make a hard right turn into the bend and away from the island. Even though the overnight raid had disabled some of the shore guns, there were still plenty of gun batteries along the Tennessee side, as well as floating batteries to harass her through the entire journey. For two days, Foote's armada hammered away at the Rebels, trying to silence as many Confederate cannons as possible.

In the meantime, sailors fortified the *Carondelet's* forward deck and pilothouse with planks, chains, and whatever else they could find. They also tied a barge, filled with stacks of hay bales, to her left side. This was to absorb the cannonballs shot at her exposed flank as she steamed past the Rebel batteries. Engineers did their best to muffle her steam engines that could give away her position in the dark. They did this by rerouting the exhaust from the smokestacks to the rear of the ship.

She was ready by Friday, April 4, to make the run. The promise of an evening storm offered the clandestine conditions Foote had been waiting for. At dusk, twenty sharpshooters, on loan from the army, boarded the ship and took positions around the deck to harass enemy gun crews. At 10 o'clock, the sailors dashed all the lights aboard and cast off her mooring lines. She was underway.

Navigator First Master William Hoel held his breath as he watched his helmsman steer past the shore battery that their comrades had supposedly disabled just three nights before. Not a sound came from them. Commander Walke patted him on the shoulder, "Well, that's the first test tonight, Bill." Hoel let his breath ease out of him.

The sharpshooters on the deck strained to see into the darkness as they chugged towards the island. The guns there were silent. Fat drops of rain began to splat on their shoulders. The men instinctively lowered their muzzles or tucked them under their jackets to keep the water out of the barrels. Just then, flames erupted out of the smokestacks, shooting straight into the night air.

"What the hell was that?" Commander Walke asked, flinching at the sudden flash of light.

"It's the soot build up in the smokestacks, sir," Hoel said, eyes darting around the ceiling of the pilothouse. "With the steam diverted to our rear, there must not be enough dampness to keep the soot from catching on fire!"

Still, not a sound came from the enemy's guns. The men looked around frantically for any signs of enemy activity. They found none. Just as a sailor let out a sigh of relief, a second burst of flames shot from the stacks. "Jesus Christ! Why the hell weren't the flue caps left open?!" Walke demanded. No one had a chance to answer. Rockets lurched into the sky from the Rebel shore. Cannons belched fire into the darkness. "Engines full steam!" Walke shouted. The Tennessee shore once again exploded in fire. Cannonballs came screaming overhead.

"They're over-shooting us!" one of the sailors yelled. The Federal ships behind them began to return fire in support. Mortar shells screamed overhead back towards the Rebel guns. The *Carondelet* chugged on. Sailors on the bow had to drop weighted lines into the water to test the depth. Then they shouted back their findings to the pilot house. It was the only way the navigator could feel their way through the inky darkness. A flash of lightning suddenly revealed that they were mere yards from crashing into the island, the guns there were clearly visible.

"Hard a-port!" Hoel screamed to his helmsman. The ship turned hard to the right just in time to avoid beaching herself on the island.

"There she is!" a southern voice shouted mere yards away in the darkness. "Fire!" The Rebels fired off a barrage at near point blank range, but the cannonballs sailed overhead, just missing the smokestacks. The *Carondelet* slipped back into the darkness and steamed away from the island. She had made it through.

Carl was sitting with his tent mates near their campfire the next morning. He was trying to dry out his uniform after a night of drenching rain. They could hear cannons booming on the river and men cheering along the shore. The cheering got louder and louder as the crowd of spectators grew. Finally, he and others from his company got up and joined the crowd. They elbowed their way through to see what was happening. Across the water was a big black monstrous boat firing on the Rebel shore batteries. It looked like some kind of giant metal turtle belching huge clouds of hideous black smoke into the air.

"What in the world is that thing?" Chucky stared with his mouth agape.

"That, boys, is our ticket across the river," Captain Newman said as he came up from behind, placing his hands on their shoulders. "The Navy'll be sending another one soon. Once they clear out those Rebel guns it'll be our turn."

The rest of H Company started to gather around their captain. He squatted down to draw a map in the dirt with a stick. "The river to the west and Reelfoot Lake with its surrounding swamps to the east create a narrow strip of land between Island No. 10 to the north and Tiptonville to the south. Once the Navy starts their assault on the island, the fleeing Rebels will have to pass through that strip to escape. That or swim for their lives. The transports will dump us here at Watson's Landing. We'll be right in their path to bag them as they come," he said, looking back up at his troops with a smile. "It'll be like shooting fish in a barrel, boys."

Two night's later the *Pittsburg* made her run, unscathed. She joined the *Carondelet* in destroying Rebel shore batteries the very next day. In the meantime, Pope's army drilled and prepared for the crossing and the fight that would follow. Carl saw little of Klaus in those days. After their previously interrupted duel, the one-handed German was too busy with his staff duties to settle any personal scores. Carl was thankful for that, but he worried that the matter would have to be addressed once again soon. That is, if both of them survived the impending assault.

He worried about his friends on the other side too. Did Kyle survive the weeks of Federal bombardment? Did he get in trouble when he returned to duty? Would he have to face him in battle? He wondered about Kathryn and Liza too. Did they make it home? Clearly, the Rebel cavalry lieutenant that he and Elijah tied up must have known the girls were in on the scheme. Would that lead back to Kyle? Carl let out a sigh as he watched the ironclad gunboats do their work on the Rebel batteries. Once again, he thought about the beautiful Kathryn and what it was like to touch her, to kiss her. He felt he could smell her faintly on the wind. He pulled the locket from his trousers and looked at the picture of Anna. It was the only thing he could do to break the spell.

The transports and barges started to emerge from Saint Johns Bayou at New Madrid. The newly dug canal allowed them to bypass the guns at Island No. 10. The next morning, Brigadier General Paine and his division loaded on to them and made the crossing. Silently, they watched the enemy shore, waiting for the barrage of cannons that surely must be ready to greet them. The only thing that greeted them was an old black man from the Watson farm. He waved to them as they disembarked onto the remnants of a ruined shore battery that had been there.

"Where's your master?" General Paine asked him.

"Done run off into the swamp...scared to death," the old man said, pointing back behind himself with his thumb.

"I see," Paine said, taking in the scene of ruined cannons and destroyed fortifications.

"I could make you some coffee," the old man said, pulling Paine from his reverie.

Paine regarded the old man and his kind warm eyes for a moment, "Um...sure, that would be great, please."

The transports returned to New Madrid to pick up the next wave of men. Paine organized his division on the Tennessee shore and started marching them to Tiptonville. The road was cluttered with discarded equipment and hastily abandoned camps. The army marched on, catching glimpses of fleeing Rebel forces, but for the most part, they took in prisoners as hungry looking men came out of the woods with their hands in the air.

By 8 o'clock the next morning, the remaining Confederate troops who hadn't managed to escape into the surrounding swamps were formed up in Tiptonville's town center. A larger formation of Federal troops surrounded them. Carl watched as the Confederate Brigadier General, William Mackall, handed his sword to General Paine and then offered a stiff salute. Paine returned the salute, then offered his hand. The two men shook hands, speaking kind words to each other. Paine placed his other hand on Mackall's shoulder in an act of friendship.

The Southern soldiers then took turns stacking their arms, some of which were old flintlocks and squirrel guns. The men were thin and shivered in their shabby worn uniforms. Some wore nothing much more than blankets wrapped around them. Some were mere boys that couldn't have been more than 12 or 13 years old. Carl pitied them as he scanned their faces. He was looking for Kyle but didn't see him.

He went to the landing after the surrender ceremony to watch the prisoners load onto the same transports that had carried the Federal troops across the river just the day before. He searched the sea of thin, dejected faces but could not find his friend among them. Carl rode back to Tiptonville. Men were still coming out of the swamps with their hands in the air, trading themselves in for a hot meal and a warm blanket. Still, Carl found no sign of Kyle.

Carl heard moans and cries coming from a hospital tent set up just on the edge of town. Dozens of sick, wounded, and dying Rebel soldiers were crammed inside. A large woman with rolled up sleeves and a blood-splattered apron regarded Carl with contempt as he ducked inside. In her hand was a bloody saw. A second woman, with her back to him, was holding in-place the thigh of an unconscious man. The first woman started sawing away just below his knee. Carl looked away quickly, regretting having witnessed the bloody scene.

He tried to ignore the sawing sound as well as the moans and cries of the ailing men as he went down the rows looking for his friend. He let out a startled yelp when a hand reached out and grabbed his wrist. Carl looked down to see a bleary-eyed, tear-stained face look up at him in fury.

"Why are you here?" the man groaned in agony.

Carl looked down at the face, which was distorted with anger and pain, "I...I don't know," Carl mumbled in bewilderment. The man's face twisted even more in agony as he let out a scream in pain. Carl tried to pull his hand away, but the man had it locked in an iron grasp. "Ma'am, this man is in pain!" Carl called out to the big woman. "Can't you do something?!"

"You Yankees done already killed that one. We've got to work on the ones we can save. If you haven't noticed, I'm a little busy right now," she said looking up from the bloody work she and her assistant were doing.

The man let out another scream in agony, digging his dirty nails into Carl's arm. "Don't you have anything for the pain?" Carl asked in desperation.

"Why don't you go ask one of your fancy Yankee doctors? We only have enough ether to work on the ones we can save. Now will you please leave me to my work, sir?!" she said blowing a strand of bangs from her mouth.

Determined to help, Carl tried to peel himself away from the dying man, but the man's grip was unbreakable. Instead, the man pulled Carl's hand to his own dirty face. The man looked up at Carl with tears streaming from his eyes, his face distorted in pain. "Please…please, don't leave me…" he gasped. Carl looked down at him with wide-eyed bewilderment. "Please, don't leave me…" the man sobbed.

Carl opened his fingers and threaded them through the man's hair. "I won't," he said, now looking down at the man in pity, "I promise." The Rebel soldier held Carl's hand close to his cheek and cried softly with his eyes closed. Carl stood there and watched as the sobs got quieter and quieter. The man slowly drifted from consciousness. Carl watched his chest rise and fall, at first in deep drafts, and then it slowed, softer and softer, until he moved no more.

Carl caressed the dead man's hair. For the first time, the man's face looked at peace. He was a young man that seemed to be at the height of his potential. "Rest easy, my friend," Carl murmured. He had to peel the dead man's fingers off his hand to break free from his grip. The smells of sick men and their body fluids were overwhelming. The women continued to work among the moaning and screaming men. Carl felt light-headed. He stumbled his way out of the tent as the women looked at him one more time and shook their heads.

Outside the town was abuzz with military activity. Prisoners were still being processed and marched off to the transports, their breath making clouds of vapors as they trudged through the mud. General Paine moved through the town on his horse surrounded by his staff. A woman stepped in front of him. "They are stealing my chickens, General," she said pointing indiscriminately at the soldiers coming and going behind her, "I shan't have one left!"

"I'm exceedingly sorry, ma'am," Paine said, looking down at her, "but we are going to put down this rebellion if it takes every chicken in Tennessee." He kicked his horse and rode off with his staff, leaving the woman to stand in the mud, her mouth open in outrage. Carl let out a chuckle which caused her to immediately snap her attention to him.

"I'm sorry, ma'am," Carl said, suddenly embarrassed.

"Hmph!" she offered in return and stormed off.

Carl stood there in the mud watching the scene around him. He let out a sigh. Kyle had to be alive somewhere. He just knew it.

…This story continues in The Perils of Perryville, available now!

Did you like it? Please give me a review on Amazon, goodreads, or anywhere else and Please, join the Engdahl House email list for updates on new releases, discounts, appearances, and more at:

https://subscribepage.io/EngdahlHouse.

Historical Note

Thank you for reading the first book of what will be a trilogy and possibly more. I, myself, am a great fan of historical fiction. You and I have probably read a lot of the same books and are fans of the same authors. We both are probably life long students of history, even if it's mostly from the armchair for me. Because of that, I've tried to be as faithful to history as possible while spinning my fictional tale at the same time. While I won't cover every detail here, I'd like to point out a few things of note that are in my book.

Most of the main characters are fictional although there are plenty of real historical figures that you may recognize. I tried to be as faithful and respectful to them as possible. Some of their speech is my invention, sometimes I use actual quotes attributed to them. On a few occasions, I paraphrased some of their quotes to be easier read by our twenty-first-century eyes, but I tried hard to keep true to the spirit of what they were saying and their intentions.

Brigadier General Pierre Gustave Toutant-Beauregard commanded the Rebel forces that fired on Fort Sumter and officially kicked off the American Civil War. I think it's very interesting that Fort Sumter was commanded by Beauregard's old friend and teacher from West Point, Major Robert Anderson. A student firing on his teacher is just one of the many stories during the war in which friend fought against friend and family fought against family. I think those true stories, tragic as they are, are what inspired me to write this book.

Of chapter one, I can tell you that the *Code Duello* is a real book that dictated how men were to duel. Dueling was illegal in Detroit at that time, as it was in most places. So was flogging, as Carl's judge mentioned. Detroit's whipping post had been removed decades before the American Civil War.

Dr. Rosenstein used willow bark extract to treat Carl's inflamed neck. Many of you may already know that willow bark extract was a common medicine at the time. It's very similar to our modern day aspirin.

Captain Chester C. E. Newman was a real person who commanded Company H of the 2nd Michigan Volunteer Cavalry. I found very little about him other than a reference to him in Marshall P. Thatcher's memoir, *A Hundred Battles in the West: St. Louis to Atlanta, The Second Michigan Cavalry.* He describes him as wearing "a stunning hat with a feather." This detail was important enough that Thatcher felt he had to include it. I could be wrong, but it tells me of a man that is proud, confident, and full of panache. Please forgive me if you know more about him and I got him wrong. I would be very interested in learning more about the man in the "stunning hat."

Samuel Sykes & Company was a real company based out of Detroit. They were one of several that had been commissioned to make uniforms.

Sergeant George Barth, Charles Scott (who I've nick-named "Chucky"), and Max Bates are actual names I pulled from the H Company's roster. Everything else about them is my invention. If I got it wrong, or you're a descendant of one of them, I meant no disrespect. I'd love to hear their real stories.

There are accounts that the men complained about the food at Fort Anderson in Grand Rapids, including the captain that threw the fork and said, "My men shall not eat with rusty forks!" It had been supplied by local contractors.

Marshall P. Thatcher described Lieutenant Colonel William Davies in his memoirs. I haven't been able to find more about him. I'd like to know if he really did fight in the Crimean war. He seems to have an interesting history. If you know more about him, please share!

Rifle and Light Infantry Tactics by William J. Hardee was used by both sides. Hardee commanded troops for the Confederacy.

As you probably guessed, the Detroit Women's City Club was real and one of many urban women's clubs across America. They did a lot of work fundraising and providing comfort packages for our soldiers. The Detroit Women's City Club was at its peak during the First World War. Their membership started to decline after the Second World War.

The Benton Barracks is now a city park in St. Louis. Laura and I got a chance to visit. There wasn't any kind of marker we could find. Still, it was interesting to look at the grounds and imagine thousands of troops marching and drilling there. General William Tecumseh Sherman did spend a brief time there after having a nervous breakdown. General Ulysses S. Grant, however, knew Sherman was far too valuable to leave on a shelf. Sherman would eventually accept the surrender of General Joseph E. Johnston a few years later, and that would be the end of the major armed conflicts of the American Civil War.

An interesting note I'd like to add: General Johnston was so impressed with Sherman's magnanimity at the surrender that for the rest of his life he would never allow anyone to disparage him in his presence. Johnston would eventually be a pallbearer at Sherman's funeral. It's that kind of humanity that I tried to write to in this book.

The exchange between Colonel Granger and Major General John Pope on the reviewing stand went down pretty much as I described it. Granger was known for having quite a mouth on him.

The Bethune Plantation is purely fictional, as are all the characters associated with it.

General PGT Beauregard was not well when he came to Bowling Green. He was struggling with a throat ailment that had haunted him since childhood. It would eventually cause him to be bedridden for weeks. He was only beginning to recover when he had to take over command at the Battle of Shiloh, which took place right around the same time the Federals had completed their siege of Island No. 10.

I think the only thing scarier than writing about Nathan Bedford Forrest in my own politically charged time, would probably be meeting him on the battlefield in his time. Forrest is a controversial figure to this day. I can tell you that here in Tennessee, he is still considered a villain to many and a hero to some. It is not my intention to weigh in on that argument. I tried to write honestly and objectively about him. I will say that the fact that he made a living by catching runaway slaves and selling human beings before the war is despicable. So were many things men under his command did during the war, including the Massacre at Fort Pillow, which I will address in a later book. Forrest is also credited for being the first Grand Wizard of the Ku Klux Klan.

Certainly, Forrest's resume does plenty to condemn him. To be fair, I think it's important to point out that he had somewhat of a change of heart later in life. He denounced the KKK and testified against it before Congress. Although, he did admit to telling some "gentlemanly lies" to protect his friends.

In 1875 Forrest gave a speech before the Independent Order of Pole-Bearers Association, an African-American group dedicated to black rights and economic development. Forrest spoke of inter-racial unity saying:

"I want to elevate you to take positions in law offices, in stores, on farms, and wherever you are capable of going...I came to meet you as friends and welcome you to the white people. I want you to come nearer to us. When I can serve you, I will do so. We have but one flag, one country; let us stand together."

He would die two years later from complications with diabetes.

Is that enough to forgive him of his terrible past? I leave that up to you to decide for yourself.

One thing that cannot be debated is that Forrest was a brilliant military leader. There's a reason he was called the "Wizard of the Saddle." All his military exploits I've described in this book are true, including some of his dialogue, especially his reaction to the Federal ironclads approaching Fort Donelson, and his argument with his superior officers that they could easily break out of Fort Donelson before the Federals completely box them in. Much of the rest of his dialogue, especially to my fictional character, Kyle Bethune, is my own invention, although I tried to match his manner of speaking and overall personality from the sources I have.

Forrest did set an ambush against the Federals as they approached Fort Donelson and led a devastating counter-flanking maneuver that held them in place before General Buckner denied his request for support and ordered him back to the fort.

The episode in which Forrest shot a Federal sniper, or "sharpshooter" as they were called then, at 600 yards is true according to accounts at the time, as is his capturing of Federal guns during the Rebels' attempted breakout from the fort. Later, he led a daring escape from Fort Donelson, much as I described it. That escape saved many men to fight another day. Many scholars argue that he could have saved a lot more men if his commanding officers would have allowed him.

Forrest continued to fight until the very end of the war. He will certainly make a return appearance in future books of this series.

The Confederate soldier who called his shot from the parapets at Fort Donelson, and then proceeded to shoot down an ironclad's smokestack with his cannon, was Private John G. Frequa. That really happened, including the words he said. Good shot, John.

General John Buchanan Floyd had plenty to fear about surrendering to the Federals. He had been the US Secretary of War prior to the breakout of the American Civil War. Many accused him of purposely sending supplies to Federal depots in the South knowing that they would be easily snatched up by Rebel forces. Many accused him of treason. He died before the war was over and never had to face those charges.

Colonel Lucius M. Walker did command Fort Bankhead at New Madrid. He has an interesting story. He rose to the rank of Brigadier General and participated in several battles after New Madrid. He died in a duel with a fellow officer. Walker had withdrawn his troops one evening from the frontline after a battle because he feared a Federal flanking maneuver would come that night in the dark. This action left Brigadier General John S. Marmaduke's troops woefully exposed. Marmaduke called out Walker for putting his troops at risk. Walker took this as an accusation of cowardice and demanded satisfaction.

Despite orders from Major General Sterling Price that both men remain in their quarters to cool off, they met on the banks of the Arkansas River with pistols. Both missed their first round, but Marmaduke fatally wounded Walker with his second shot. Marmaduke immediately came to Walker's assistance. Walker forgave him as he lay there dying. Sadly, his wife was giving birth to their son, Lucius Marshall Walker Jr., at the same time.

My descriptions of Colonel Granger and Captain Carr's different results with the Confederate sharpshooters are pretty accurate, although Carr did make it back to the Federal lines before dying of his wounds. The Battle for New Madrid went as I described it. The Confederates slipped away in the night. When the 1st US Infantry entered Fort Thompson, they found only two Rebel soldiers who were sleeping. Why those soldiers were there, I'm not sure, so I had them be lookouts for the fleeing forces that were left behind.

The hot air balloon used to scout Island No. 10 was the only one used in the Western Theater during the war. I thought it was too interesting not to add to the story. The tornado that tore through both camps did occur. I thought it was also an interesting detail that I just had to include in my story.

The final assault on Island No. 10 and the Rebel forces on the Tennessee side went pretty much as I described it, including the *Carondelet's* daring night run past the Rebel guns. By the way, the term "hard a port" would seem like a left turn, but it actually means to turn right or *starboard*. It was an archaic phrase at the time left over from the days of tillers, even though it was still used with wheels. So "hard a-port" means to slam the tiller to the left causing the rudder to go right and therefore a right turn for the boat. I know. It's confusing, but trust me on this. Many people think it's also a mistake in the movie *Titanic* because the order was "hard a-starboard" but the helmsman turns the wheel left. It's not a mistake. It's actually pretty good attention to detail in that film.

Once the Federals crossed the river, they met very little resistance. That's because after deeming the defense of Island No. 10 a lost cause, General Beauregard pulled most of the troops and brought them to Corinth where he and General Sidney Johnston were staging an assault on the Federals encamped around Pittsburg Landing. That assault would be known as the Battle of Shiloh, the bloodiest battle in US history up to that point.

The plan for the remaining troops at Island No. 10 was to hold up Pope's army long enough for Johnston to destroy Grant's forces before Pope and Don Carlos Buell's armies could reinforce them. What the Federals ended up finding once they crossed the river, was a small token force of under-equipped and underfed men. Many of them were too sick to fight.

The exchange between General Paine and the angry woman I described did take place according to accounts. Allegedly, it was during the Federal march to Tiptonville. I moved it to the next day after the surrender ceremony in Tiptonville. I thought Paine's response was funny, although I feel bad for the woman who was losing her food source to the invading army, as I do for all the people that were affected by this terrible war, regardless of whose side they were on. I mean no disrespect to them.

Island No. 10 no longer exists today as it did during the American Civil War. Natural erosion has eaten it away over time. The river is constantly changing as it washes away some places and builds others with its silt deposits. New Madrid is still there. There's a museum in town that you can visit which has a Battle of Island No. 10 display. I plan to visit it soon. Maybe I can convince them to sell this book in their gift shop. I can only dream.

I should also mention that Reelfoot Lake has changed shape since the mid-19th century. At the time of the battle, it was long and cigar-shaped which created a natural barrier for the fleeing rebels east of the river. It has receded into more of an indefinable blob today. The Rebels may have had an easier time escaping north of the lake had it been in its current shape. The lake original formed due to the New Madrid earthquakes that occurred earlier in the century.

The war would rage on for another three years. I plan on continuing Carl and his friends' stories all the way through, as well as the real history of the 2nd Michigan Voluntary Cavalry.

Thank you so much for reading my book! I hope you stay with me through this journey. If you like, you can find me on social media, I'm on all the big ones, and please join the Engdahl House email list for updates on new releases, discounts, appearances, and more at https://subscribepage.io/EngdahlHouse.

Thanks

Cody C. Engdahl

Preview of
2nd Michigan Cavalry Chronicles:
Book 2

The Perils of Perryville

Now available!

Cold panic poured through Carl as he cowered behind his tree.

"Shoot! For God's sake, shoot, you idiots!" Captain Newman shouted as he fired his pistol into the rush of approaching men.

Like jumping off a cliff, Carl pushed himself from the tree, turned, and fired the rest of his cylinders into the rush of men with little effect. A heavily bearded man tore after him with his bayonet. Without thinking, Carl deflected the blade with the barrel of his carbine, but the man's forward motion barreled him over and soon, Carl found himself on his back with the man on top, squeezing the air out of his neck. He grabbed at the man's wrists and struggled to get free. Then he remembered his pistol. He patted his side frantically until he found it. The bearded man, sensing the new danger, turned to grab the gun. Carl fired as the man pushed his arm away causing the bullet to strike him in the shoulder.

"Aaagh! Damn it!" the man screamed as he fell off and rolled on the ground in agony clutching his shoulder. "You shot me, you son of a bitch!"

Carl scurried to his feet, holding his pistol on the man who was now reeling in pain. He looked up and saw he was surrounded by scenes of hand-to-hand fighting. Then several of the Rebels started shouting, "Fall back! Fall back!"

All around Confederate soldiers started to look up from their individual fights only to have their faces turn from fury to fear. They quickly disengaged and joined the retreat. The ground began to shake as a heavy rumble took over the sounds of fighting. Carl looked back at his opponent who had gotten to his knees. Still holding his shoulder, the man's face went white with horror. Carl turned to see the nightmare scene unfolding. Hordes of blue-clad horsemen came thundering through the woods. At the head of the column rode a man with furious blue eyes. He held the reins with his brass claw as he hacked his way through the crowd of fleeing Rebels with his saber.

"Good God…" Carl murmured at the terrifying scene.

"Hey, if you ain't gonna kill me, I'm gettin' the hell out of here," the man behind him spoke. Carl turned to see his opponent scramble off with his hand still clutching his shoulder. For a moment, the murderous sight of Klaus reaping men down like wheat gave him the urge to run too.

Glossary of terms

Abattis: an obstacle, like a felled tree used as a field fortification.

Bayonet: a long, knife-like weapon that can be attached to the end of a rifle to create a spear-like weapon.

Buckshot: a shotgun load of several pellets instead of a single bullet.

Carbine: a short rifle made for cavalry use.

Contraband: a runaway slave that follows the Union Army.

Earthwork: a tall mound of dirt piled up as a defensive wall.

Hardtack: a hard cracker-like bread issued as rations.

Mortar: a large, cauldron-shaped artillery piece that lobs shells instead of shooting directly.

Musket: a muzzleloading black powder long gun. It can be a rifle or smoothbore.

Orderly: an aide assigned to do menial tasks for officers.

Picket: a small group of men set out from the main group as a lookout or guard.

Rifle: a long gun with groves in the barrel that causes the bullet to spin. Rifles can still be muzzle-loading muskets

Saber: a single-bladed, curved sword designed for slashing from horseback

Shotgun: a smoothbore weapon that shoots multiple pellets instead of a single bullet.

<u>Skirmishers:</u> light troops set out in front of the main formation to harass the enemy.
<u>Vedette:</u> same as a picket but on horseback

Typical Civil War Military units:
<u>Company or a troop:</u> about a hundred men, but varies greatly
*<u>Battalion:</u> usually about four to five companies or half a regiment.
<u>Regiment:</u> made up of several companies, typically ten.
<u>Brigade:</u> made up of several regiments, typically three.
<u>Division:</u> made up of more than one brigades.
<u>Corps:</u> made up of more than one brigades, typically three.
<u>Army:</u> made up of several corps.

*The word battalion has replaced the word regiment in the modern US military.

<u>Enlisted Rank</u>
Private
Corporal
Sergeant
First Sergeant
Sergeant Major
<u>Officer Rank</u>
2nd Lieutenant
1st Lieutenant
Captain: Usually commands a company
Major
Lieutenant Colonel

Colonel: usually commands a regiment
Brigadier General: usually commands a brigade
Major General: usually commands a division
Lieutenant General: usually commends a corps
General: usually commands an army.

Sources

This book is a work of fiction. However, there are many historical accounts in it. I tried to stay as faithful to real history as possible. Below are some of the sources I used in my research. I highly recommend them if you want to learn more about the real history that this book is based on.

Daniel, Larry J. and Bock, Lynn N. (1996) *Island No. 10: Struggle for the Mississippi Valley.* Tuscaloosa, AL: The University of Alabama.

Thatcher, Marshall P. (1884) *A Hundred Battles in the West: St Louis to Atlanta, 1861-65, The Second Michigan Cavalry.* Detroit, MI: self-published.

civilwarpodcast.org

civilwartalk.com

historicalemporium.com

Dr. Ranney, Geo E., Surgeon 2nd Michigan Cavalry. (1897) *War papers read before the Michigan Commandery ... v.2. Military Order of the Loyal Legion of the United States. "Reminiscences of an army surgeon."* Detroit, MI: James H. Stone & Company.

Cooling, Benjamin Franklin. (1987) *Fort Henry and Donelson, The Key to the Confederate Heartland.* University of Tennessee Press.

Kidd, James Harvey. (1908) *Personal Recollections of a Cavalryman With Custer's Michigan Cavalry Brigade in the Civil War.* Ionia, MI: Sentinel Press.

Volo, Dorothy Denneen and Volo, James M. (1998) *Daily Life in Civil War America.* Greenwood Press.

Miles, Tiya. (1970) *The Dawn of Detroit: a Chronicle of Slavery and Freedom in the City of the Straits.* The New Press.

Woodford, Arthur M. (2001) *This is Detroit, 1701-2001.* Detroit, MI: Wayne State University.

Works by Cody C. Engdahl

Novels:

The Long Century Series
- Rampage on the River: The Battle for Island No. 10 (Book I)
- The Perils of Perryville (Book II)
- Blood for Blood at Nashville (Book III)
- Mexico, My Love (Book IV)
- The Prussian Prince (Book V)

Nonfiction:
- The American Civil War WAS About Slavery: A Quick Handbook of Quotes to Reference When Debating Those Who Would Argue Otherwise
- How to Write, Publish, and Market Your Novel

Please, join the Engdahl House email list for updates on new releases, discounts, appearances, and more at: https://subscribepage.io/EngdahlHouse.